ALISHA

KOHINOOR IN MY LIFE

HARISH HIREHALLI

Dedictaed to

You

Contents

Prologue

Varun and I were in the lift, on our way to the top floor, where he was staying, so we had some time to talk. To break the silence, he asked me, '*Bhai*, what next in life?' It was the last week of college.

'As usual', I answered, 'have a job, make money and get old.'

'That is everyone's story. Apart from that, what do you want to become? What have you imagined for yourself or wished for?'

'Hmmm... I would write, I guess, but I'm not sure. I have always dreamt of being a writer. I observe too much and notice little things very keenly. These instincts could be my driving force.'

He seemed surprised. 'Oh, really!'

I nodded.

'That is nice. I have noticed the way you observe little things around you. I think it comes naturally to you. It's good that you have grasped it.' Before I could say anything in response, Varun continued. 'Have you written anything till now?'

'Yes, I have.'

That seemed to have gotten him surprised again, because he knew me very well; I just say things most of the time, but I do not generally act on them, so his shock was not unfounded.

He immediately asked me to show what I had written.

Before sharing it with him, I stated two conditions.

Condition 1: I wanted an honest review.

It was my first attempt. It was not a complete story yet, and I had just written a tiny bit. I was also not sure whether

I had it in me. Varun was the perfect guy to ask for an honest review, as he was an excellent student, the best in sports, and A typical guy that any girl would have liked to date.

Condition 2: this I would reveal once he was done reading the story.

He agreed to it, and I forwarded the file to him.

Meanwhile, we reached his room and started preparing for the final exam of our college life. We revised some important questions, as we had only two hours left for it.

During the last thirty minutes, we went to the mess to have our lunch. This was a crucial period, because we would discuss what we had read so far while filling our empty stomach. It was this moment that would decide our level of preparation and confidence. After that, we rushed to our respective examination hall.

There is usually a gap of a few minutes after the invigilator has distributed the answering sheet and we have to wait till the sound of the siren. This gap is where everyone indulges in wishful thinking.

Some think about partying.

Some think about the career that lies ahead.

Some think about how their lives will be beyond the shelter of college.

The list goes on. I on the other hand was thinking about a girl, pondering whether I should confess to her or not!

Soon, the siren sounded, and the invigilator gave us the question paper, wishing us all the very best for our final exam.

Within no time, people started walking out after submitting their answers. I couldn't help wondering how fast they could write. Eventually, I also walked out for one last time.

After finishing the test, I went to our *adda called Kailasha Chai Center*; we met on a regular basis and had tea together it was the only place where we used to drink Tea and doing it from day one to today. There she was, standing all alone, waiting for all of us to arrive.

I was on the other side of the road. Seeing me, she waved her hand. I smiled and waved back, walking towards her. She gave me a hug and asked me how the exam was.

'It was okayish. I will pass for sure. Tea?' I went to get chai. '*Anna*, two tea *kodi* (Please serve two cups of tea).'

From behind I heard, 'Karna, order two more.' I turned around. There was Varun and Nikil. The *chaiwallah bhai* got the hint. 'Four tea, *na*?'

'Yes.'

We were all discussing tonight's plan while sipping hot tea, perhaps for the last time. Every day for two years, this had been our custom – drinking tea together during break and making plans for the night when we would disperse from here, not knowing that one day these moments will come to an end. How beautiful those days were, and how we would miss being here together with these people who made this journey such a memorable one!

CHAPTER I

WHAT'S HER NAME?

That night, we all went to a fancy pub named *Lord of the Drinks* in Koregaon Park, Pune. We drank like animals; half credit should go to Zomato Gold, which saved us a few bucks and got us an extra buzz. We danced like no one was watching, excluding me, for it takes four or five pints of beer for me to acquire that courage; even two LIITs would work. I dance awfully, but with Prajwal, Madhu and Nikil around, it feels like there are people who dance worse than me. Of course, with the steps of Varun and *that girl*, my confidence fails me. Prajwal and I just copied their moves. We were having an amazing night. Everyone was exhausted when the DJ shouted, 'Come on, party people, last song of the night on its way!' All of a sudden, our packets of energy burst, and we began dancing again with all our crazy might. When the song ended, all the folks in the pub started shouting.

'One more song! One more song!'

And we all joined in the chant. One more song!

The DJ considered the mob's request and played an Avicii song, announcing that it was this song that was his inspiration to become DJ. 'Here we go, folks. Enjoy the night!' The beats started to drop, and so did our dance moves.

We paid our bills and booked the cab, which was waiting near the pub.

I reminded Varun, '*Bhai*, don't forget to read that story that I sent.'

He replied, 'I will read and give you your honest review. But I am curious about your second condition!'

'Only if you ask me the right question! And I am sure you will get there.'

This sparked his curiosity and seemed to challenge him. 'And what would that be?'

Meanwhile, our cab arrived. *That girl* and Prajwal were going to go to our apartment, and the others were going to the hostel, so they were waiting for their cab to arrive. We said bye to everyone and left. When he reached home, a sleepy Rohan answered the door, straightaway throwing himself back on the bed.

Oh! I forgot to tell you about Rohan and Prajwal. Rohan was my roommate, and Prajwal lived with his family but would mostly stay in our home. It was a two-BHK, but all of us used to sleep in one room. There was one properly maintained bed, which belonged to the girl, and on the other two beds, which remained messy, it was me, Prajwal and Rohan.

She was tired, so she went to bed right away. Prajwal and I went to the balcony, as he wanted to smoke. I was excited about the story that I had written and couldn't wait for Varun's response, so I insisted that Prajwal read it to see how he would react. I opened the file on my phone and handed it to him.

'What is this, "The Fear"?'

'Go on, read it,' I urged, not telling him that I was the writer.

He started to read.

The Fear

Do you ever feel the tension when someone you like, or love, the most goes out with the one you hate – well, not exactly hate but let's just say you wouldn't want that person to cross your path?

If you have, my story will make you recall that moment.

When I found out about her meeting plans with that guy for the first time, I could not get rid of the thought from my mind. I felt low and anxious; it was a different kind of fear, where my mind felt disconnected from the rest of my body, which you wouldn't be able to express in words. It's like, everything around feels ominous. I was afraid that she was slipping away from me, and I couldn't do much, because if I expressed how I felt about her, I might lose what I had.

They say, 'The danger of losing something stimulates us much more than the prospect of making a similar gain.'

That day, I came back to my room and tried all sorts of things to get distracted, but I couldn't because the thought of her affected me so much that I would inevitably come back to obsessing about her.

I realised she played a vital role in my life. I didn't know what this feeling was called. Perhaps it's what both you and I are thinking right now.

'Love.'

Am I in love?

Well, I really don't know what the definition of love is, but according to my limited experience in that field, I can say:

Love is such a beautiful emotion that it has all the power in the world, which makes us strive to do impossible things to put a smile on the faces of our loved ones.

Whether it be bringing coffee to them early in the morning or travelling miles just to wish them a happy birthday.

I couldn't even sleep that day.

It happened for the first time after a long time. My eyes could rest only after being touched by the early morning light. I woke up at around 10 AM and immediately checked my mobile for her text or call.

The disappointment was waiting for me with a wicked smile on her face, saying, '*Soh jaa beta, kuch nahin hai yahaan* (Go to sleep, son, there is nothing here).'

My mind started racing in the opposite direction. *Dude, stop thinking about her. She doesn't care much about you. Plus, you don't fit in her league. You don't know how to dance, you're not that good looking and you suck at expressing your feelings for her.*

But deep down, I could see a ray of hope that all she needed was love from someone who cared for and loved her as her parents did. Once she found out about my good intentions, it would be a matter of cakewalk for me.

But the question was, *how do I make her see my good parts?*

That day, I waited an eternity for notification with her name on it. I had only heard of a minute feeling like hours in movie dialogues; I had laughed about them, sniggering that this was all bullshit, but it all makes sense now. It all happens in real life.

After a while, her name flashed on my screen, and my heartbeat started to accelerate with a flood of relief. It was a moment more satisfying than the time I had cleared my backlog in engineering mathematics.

Prajwal asked me, 'Is it written by you?'

'Yes!' I answered excitedly.

No sooner had I said yes than he shot his next question. 'What's her name?'

I said, 'Will tell you the complete story tomorrow. Both of us are tired now. Let's go to sleep.'

But he wasn't taking no for an answer, so I had to give him something and make him settle for it. As he was drunk, I assumed the alcohol was doing the talking.

I said, 'You know her', and before he could respond, I said 'No more questions.' He was in no state to agree because the hint made him more curious than earlier.

But I went straight to bed, and after some time, he also entered the room. 'Don't think too much about it,' I told him. 'Goodnight.'

CHAPTER II

WHAT'S HER NAME (2)

I was having a dream where I was dancing with the most beautiful woman in the world, her tiny hand wrapped under my palm, her other hand behind my back. As I was holding her, I was wearing a tuxedo while she was in a green-coloured dress, with loose hair perfectly curled, covering one of her eyes. Tucking the hair strand behind her ear, I had the chance to gaze upon her adorably round, glistening eyes. I lost myself in them. It was like being hypnotized all of a sudden with nobody around us. We were dancing hand in hand like in Hollywood rom-coms. It was as perfect as perfect could be.

Suddenly, I jumped courtesy of a continuously buzzing tone. Everything vanished – the dance, the music and even the perfect woman herself. I was surrounded by an accosting beeping sound.

I woke up.

It was a message notification that cost me that wonderful dream. I was inclined to be damn pissed at the person who was texting me.

But it was Varun, and he never texts unnecessarily. On seeing his name, my temper subsided. I opened WhatsApp Chat and started reading the messages that went like this:

Varun: *Bhai, I read the story.*

The story is promising, but frankly, you need to work on your writing skills.

Sorry if this sounds rude, but you wanted me to be honest.

So I have got one suggestion and one question.

The suggestion is that you need to improve your writing.
You have written it the way you talk.
But talking and writing are different.
And...
The question is about the story. I need to have a chat with you!
Who else have you shown this to?

I was tensed and had hardly gotten back to my senses from the previous night's hangover. I skipped to the washroom, splashed my face, drank water and went to the balcony with my mobile.

I was wondering what to tell him, debating whether I should tell him about the whole scenario or just beat around the bush.

Occupied with these thoughts, I typed my reply to him.
Me: *First of all, thank you for being frank. I wanted*
you to be frank here.
And about this, I have shown it to a few people.
But why do you ask that?
Varun: *In 'few', are there any girls included?*
Me: *Yes!!!* (I was lying here just to play safe.)
Varun: *Who all?*
Me: *Snehal, Disha and so on. But why do you*
ask?
Varun: *How was their reaction?*
Me: *Most of them were like 'Awwwww, so touching.' And*
they asked me to work on grammar.
Varun: *Why do I get the feeling that you are lying?*
And I also feel this story is real. You have written about
what you have experienced.
Don't lie to me!
Me: *It was written long ago when I was in hostel,*
after internship.

Varun: *So, you are saying it might be true, or is it?*
I am not pointing out any girl here.
But you have surely experienced what you've written.
Me: *Okay, you got me there.* (This seemed like a safe answer since I neither wanted to lie nor tell the truth.)
Unfortunately, it is true, and
I fucking felt terrible that day!
I did not want anyone to know how I felt and don't
want anyone to know her name.
So please don't ask what her name is.
Varun: *Okay, I won't ask her name, but I will tell you*
one thing. You should go and tell that
girl about your feelings.
Me: *The train has passed now, I can't anymore.*
Varun: *Go catch it before it reaches its destination.* (Clichés come to the rescue in times of crisis, or so it seemed.)
Me: *A similar kind of situation happened in the past*
when I was confused between love and friendship. I confessed
to her, and from that moment till now, she hasn't talked to me.
I ended up losing my best friend there, so I don't want that to repeat itself.
Varun: *Are you confused here also?*
Me: *Not that I am confused between love and friendship. I have known*
what I feel for her from the day we started to know each other.
Varun: *Think of it like this: she lost a good man like you.*
And you have better friends now.
You have to evolve in life. You can't be
the same person every day and to everyone.

Me: *Don't know what's wrong with me.*

I will always be the second-best in most people's life.

(This is the hard truth. Nobody remembers the second person. Only a few of them do maybe. Here is the proof: can you answer who the second person to step on the moon is?)

Varun: *If she was still with you (as friends) even after your confession, then that's the girl you want to be with.*

That's the kind of friendship you deserve.

People change, Karna... So with time, you have to become smarter in dealing with people.

Me: *What if, after my confessing, she doesn't want to talk to me?*

I can't lose one more friend.

Varun: *What if you lose her even if you don't tell her? Then what do you do?*

Me: *I am pretty sure this will happen sooner or later.*

Varun: *Then what are you waiting for?*

Me: *Till that happens from her side, I want to be with her.*

Varun: *You will be the sufferer. They'll be out of your life and*

they'll not even give a shit about you.

If you lose her now, you will at least know that you were the reason for your own loss.

Later, you will be thinking about what went wrong each time,

and it will be harder.

Me: *I will suffer for a while, but as of now, I am determined that it happen*

this way. I believe it won't hurt that much.

Varun: *If you have already made up your mind, well and good.*

Me: *Sometimes I wonder what it takes to get her. I have done*

all the things in the world for her.

People don't find my worth unless they lose me!

Varun: *Never think that. It will harm you, not her.*

Life goes on even if you and I aren't here.

It goes the same for everyone.

Most girls like to take advantage of men wanting them.

You think they don't know until you tell them, but

they always know, and yet they pretend.

Me: *True! Sometimes I feel she knows about me.*

Anyway, I end up deciding I am too good for her.

It gives me some positivity.

Varun: *But still, you try for her. And about being too good for her,*

that's the reason men will always be men!

Me: *Okay, I might tell her if the situation leads to it.*

Varun: *That's better.*

Me: *Thank you,* bhai, *and don't say anything about this to others.*

Varun: *I won't. And I was going to Anna Idli's for breakfast. Want to join?*

Me: *Yes! See you there, bye.*

When I reached the breakfast place, he was already waiting there, and as I parked my bike, I could see him smiling from the corner of my eye. Finally, I looked at him. 'What you are laughing about?'

He just shrugged. I wanted to hear the reason but didn't want to confront him all over again. 'Okay', I said, 'come, we will eat *podi idli* today.' Both of us had a good Sunday brunch, drank filter coffee – the best in Pune (which usually reminds us about Bangalore) – and then went near the college entrance. 'When is your flight?' I asked him.

'It's at 4, which means I'll be leaving at 1.'

'Okay then. I will be here at 12.'

'Don't be late, and by the way, get those drunk buggers with you. They're still sleeping, I guess.'

'Yeah, sure, they will be here on time.'

'Fine then, see you later, bye.' Varun went to the hostel to get his packing done.

I was on my way to wake up the 'drunk buggers'. On the way, I went to the grocery store to buy milk and cigarettes for Prajwal. By the time I reached home, everyone was up and hooked to their phones. I made tea for all. The girl and Rohan were drinking tea in the room, and Prajwal and I went to the balcony with our cigarettes and tea. After finishing that, we got ready and left for the hostel.

Varun was bidding farewell to his cricket team. As soon as we saw him, we called out his name. We were all a bit emotional, as he was the first guy from our group who was leaving. You must already know how it feels. Everything around had a different vibe as if they had all acquired a different shade of colour. The weather was perfect, but there were tears in the girl's eyes. Varun was giving her a hug and consoling her, as he was her favourite person. Prajwal was gesturing for me to make a video of it so that we could look at it later on.

Meanwhile, his cab arrived. We helped him load his luggage, and finally, the time came to say the last goodbye. We were all overwhelmed, but unlike the girl, we suppressed our tears.

We watched the cab till it passed the college gate. Suddenly, the cab stopped, and Varun's face popped out from the window. 'Karna, come here,' he called. I thought he must have left something behind, so I scurried to him.

'*Bhai*', he said, 'I know which girl you were referring to earlier. It's Alisha, right?'

With a huge, helpless grin on my face, I nodded.

'You still have time. Don't think about the consequences. Take her out for dinner, or plan something romantic, and confess how you feel about her.'

'Thank you so much, *bhai*, I can't express how happy I am right now.'

'Now act normal, and give this letter to the warden. I had kept it so I could have a moment with you.' He was one smart boy.

He wished me luck again and left, leaving me with an excited wing for my feelings to fly.

When I went back to them, Alisha asked why Varun had called me. I showed her the letter, which she started reading. My heart fluttered looking at her engaged in this simple act, and my happiness knew no bounds. She gave the letter back and informed me that the warden was standing a few feet away. After I had submitted the letter, we went to the café.

CHAPTER III

THE PILOT EPISODE

It was the first day of our college. I and sai were in the back seat of the auditorium listing to boring talks.

'Why are all official welcoming addresses are so boring?' complained the person sitting next to sai and me.

I replied, 'Yeah man, this guy is boring us even more compared to the previous one.'

'Makes me want to skip the after-lunch session. What say?'

I glanced at him and nodded. 'Cool, let's skip then.'

His face was stretched in a wide smile. 'I am Nikil.'

'Karna. And this is my friend Sai. He was my engineering classmate, and here we're together too.'

'*Waah*, that's nice.'

'Where are you from?' Sai asked Nikil.

'Bagalkote, Karnataka.'

and I said in unison, 'Kandavra?'

Nikil beamed. 'Yes! And you guys are from Karnataka, I assume?' he asked in English. This was weird because if one *Kannadiga* meets another *Kannadiga*, they start speaking in Kannada. But Nikil didn't. Both of us were baffled.

Sai was excited as he generally was. '*Hu guru, kannadavre* (Yes, dude, from Karnataka). *Yav college* (Which college)?'

'PES Bangalore, and schooling from Lions School, Bijapur.' Both Sai and I had heard of that school. Sai interrogated him further.

'Which year did you pass out in?'

'2010.'

'Would you by any chance know Payal?'

Nikil chirped. 'Oh, yeah, the one who was more of a boy than a girl.'

'Well, the earth is a small place after all,' I said. I started laughing looking at Sai. We didn't doubt Nikil's observation. It was a perfect explanation. The girl we were referring to, or the 'boy' tied up in a girl's body, was Sai's ex-girlfriend and my friend.

'I am missing something here,' Nikil said. 'Why are you laughing? And why is Sai shaking his head? Something is up here. Tell me!'

'I am laughing about the way in which you described her. And he is shaking his head since she was his girlfriend.' I made air quotes at the last word.

'Oh! I am sorry, bro. I didn't know that she was…'

'It's okay, man, there's nothing to say sorry about.'

The three of us cleared out the air of discomfort and became friends in no time. Meanwhile, the guy finished his boring lecture. And soon it was lunch break. We headed towards the mess, where there was a buffet system, and stood in queue. Sai and Nikil were ahead of me, and there was a girl standing behind me. Her phone suddenly rang. 'Hello,' she said. '*Amma iga uta madka bandevi* (I have just come to have lunch).'

The three of us turned to look, because she was speaking in Kannada. Nikil and Sai were quick enough to start a conversation with her. I, on the other hand, was shy as always and stood quietly. Sai introduced me to her, and all I could say was a quiet 'Hi.'

'*Nimda yav uru* (Which city are you from)?'

'Hubli,' I managed to say.

'Oh, nice. I did my 12th there. Chethana Pu College.'

'*Nanu alle hatra dale* Dharwad (I also did it near Dharwad).'

'Ah, nice,' she smiled.

This was all the conversation that I could exchange with the new girl, but Sai and Nikil were the complete opposite. They kept talking, and it soon seemed like we had already formed a group between us.

I could only stare at her face. Everything around me seemed to have blurred, and all I could fathom was her lips moving; there was complete silence around me. See, that's where the problem began; it was almost love at first sight. But it was not. I wonder why it doesn't happen usually. If it had happened then, we would be celebrating our third-year anniversary. But here I am, writing and hoping for a perfectly planned happy ending.

We had planned on skipping the second session, but that did not happen. You know the reason. Yes, you guessed it. It was the girl; she was not interested in skipping. Boys being boys, we attended that session with her. After finishing the session, we went outside instead of going to the mess. Near the main gate, we had some *vada pav*, and she reminded us about the Kannada people's meeting.

Nikil replied, 'Yeah, I saw the messages on WhatsApp. We are to meet at 6.'

'You guys are coming, right?' she asked.

'Yeah, we will be there at 6 sharp,' Sai replied on our behalf.

'*Chalo*, I have to go. See you there. Bye,' she left, waving. We headed back to our room.

There were only four colleges in India, so ours had people from different states and different culture. When the freshers, the first-year students, join college, their respective seniors, especially if they are from the same state, would arrange a 'fresher's meet' to ensure that the students bond well with each other.

As it had been a few days already, we wanted to get to know our seniors and make some new friends. Most importantly, if there was any girl from our state, then that would be great. These were the thoughts that were running in the minds of every guy. But we felt lucky since we already knew a girl.

At around 5.30, we went to the mess to have tea. Nikil introduced Sai and me to his neighbour, Varun. He was also from Karnataka. After having snacks, with a teacup in hand, we came out and headed towards the café, where people had already gathered, including a few seniors. We joined in the hub, waiting for our seniors to start. My eyes were eagerly searching for Alisha.

Meanwhile, the seniors began their speech, and everyone introduced themselves one by one. What was first a gathering of ten people grew to include half a century of them. As the introductions were happening, the girl I was searching for came out of the mess with a cup in her hand. She was looking confused as to which group was her familiar Karnataka group, because there were other groups, of other states, which had also scheduled their meeting today. Some other girl waved her hand and signalled for her to join us fast. She threw her tea in the dustbin and approached the group. Everyone was looking at her when a senior broke in.

'*Illi nodra! Amle avaln nodvantri inna two years idea nimma hatra* (Guys, attention here, please, you can watch her later. You have two years for that.)'

Everyone started laughing although she seemed a bit uncomfortable with all of the unsolicited attention on her.

To ease the moment, the seniors started with her asking to introduce herself to everyone. 'But it should be in Kannada. If even one word is in English, you would have to start all over again.'

She stood in the middle.

'*Nanna haesru Alisha* (My name is Alisha). *Nannau* shivmogga *nind bandidaeni* (I have come from Shivmogga). *Mattu nanu engineering* Mysore *nind madidaeni* (I completed my engineering from Mysore).'

'*Oh ho*, you just said "engineering." Not a Kannada word. From the start again please,' teased the senior.

It took three attempts for her to finally do the introduction as she had been asked.

Once she was done, she quickly went to the side, looking relieved.

Similarly, everyone started to introduce themselves. Eventually, the senior said, 'There are two important things here that you need to pay attention to. One is placement. Get placed as soon as possible. Second, think of this place less as a college and more as a home but without restrictions, so make the most of it. Enjoy your time here in these two years. Thanks for coming.'

Later, Nikil, Sai, Varun and I decided to go out for dinner near High Street which is IT HUB area where a lots of Fancy pubs and some quick-service restaurants along with fine dining out kind ones. we asked her to join us. She agreed, and we all had a scrumptious dinner along with some beer. There was a lot of chatter going on, but I, sitting beside her, didn't speak at all, only smiled whenever our eyes met. By the time I chugged adequate beer to get the confidence of speaking to her, she had already figured out that I am a shy person, so she took the lead. We spoke for a long time, with her making me feel comfortable with every new topic. We all got to know each other a bit more, and by the end of the night, there was less hesitation in me when it came to speaking to her.

Later that night, after we had gone back to our rooms, I texted her, saying thanks for making me feel comfortable: *I am a shy person initially. Sometimes it gets awkward and boring with me for new people, but you made it so easy for me. Thank you for coming to dinner.*

Her reply read: *I figured. No issues. Glad that you could open up with me.*

I was so happy that she and I had become friends that I probably slept like a baby that night.

CHAPTER IV

HEAP TO MOUNTAIN

As the days passed, we became better friends, and it was basically a Kannada people's group, with me, Varun, Nikil, Sai and Madhu, who was new and also from Karnataka. We used to hang out after college in the canteen and during college hours in the mess. Meanwhile, she had become friends with a few seniors too, so in the initial days of our friendship, she used to be here and there.

In Pune, there are several historical forts around, and Varun was interested in trekking, so he made the plans. I readily agreed when I found out and didn't bother asking who else would be joining us. He asked me to be ready early that weekend. That night, I found out that Sai and Nikil were also coming.

On the day we were to leave, I went to the parking lot, Gate No. 1, near Kailasha Chai Center. It was where Varun had asked us to meet. When I reached, Varun was already there waiting for us to arrive. He informed me that Madhu would also be joining us.

The Five of us viz me, madhu, varun, sai and nikil were going to Tung Fort near Lonavala. We reached around 8 in the morning and had breakfast on the way. With that, we were all set for the trek. The level of difficulty was medium, and it was going to be a long trek for beginners. It was fun till we reached halfway. As the sun started to hit our heads, it suddenly was not fun anymore. Somehow, we finally made it to the top of the fort. The view from there, along with the cool wind under the hot sun, gave me a different type of happiness, like I was in the sky and nothing around me had ever felt so peaceful.

As we reached the top, we got the signal back on our phones, so I quickly took a photo of the view that stretched before me and posted a 'story' on Instagram. Within minutes, my phone started to ring. It was Alisha. I looked apprehensively at Varun. *Bhai*, did you ask Alisha for this trek?' He shook his head. 'I thought she had plans with seniors.'

I was sceptical before answering since I was in a dilemma, so I received the call and said hello in a lower tone.

There, at that very moment, was the start of a beautiful yet painful journey of my life.

Here are a few reasons why it was *beautiful yet painful*.

#1: Emotion

She didn't say a word for a while and suddenly started sobbing. 'You guys left me, she began. 'You didn't even say a word about the plan. I would have expected you at least to call me and ask about it. But even you disappointed me.'

I was worried, but at the same time, I was happy. This was special for me. But in Zakir Khan's style, '*Waise toh main sakth launda hoon* (I am stoic when it comes to girls), *par yahaan main pigal gaya* (but here I melted).' I had never gotten this close to a girl in such a short period of time, but here was a girl who felt comfortable enough with me to cry about the hurt she felt. Out of all the people she knew, she had called me. It was very special, and it was the first time that something like this had happened. I tried to console her, insisting that she stop crying. But I was making it worse, as I had no idea how to deal with tears, but after a few apologies and promises of never letting this happen again, I was able to convince her. She stopped crying, and I said, 'I will come and meet you as soon as we come back and take you out for dinner.' She seemed embarrassed, saying that she must have overreacted a bit. I asked her not to worry. After all, it was my fault, so I told her I would make it up to her. That seemed to have cheered her up.

After some time, we left the fort and had lunch at around 4 on the way back to the hostel. Ever since the call, all I could think of was how to make up for my negligence. Dinner was there, but I wanted something more, so when we reached college, I dropped Nikil at the hostel and went to get her chocolates. I got around fifteen chocolates for her, right from the one-rupee Cadbury to the 150-rupee Silk. I called her to meet me near the cafeteria. She arrived within five minutes. I was ecstatic; it was the second time that day that I was feeling a happiness that I could feel within my soul.

'I'm so sorry,' I said. 'We thought you had other plans, so we didn't consider you in ours.'

'Chill,' she smiled. 'I am over that. There are still more weekends to come. We can all go the next time.'

We had tea and went for a walk on the campus. I told Alisha again that I felt guilty for making her cry. 'And for that, you have to take this,' I gave her the one-rupee chocolate.

She laughed. 'Aww, that's so sweet!'

After a few steps, I produced another one, and then the next, and the next, and so on, till I finally handed her the Silk.

Her eyes were wide with surprise while her cheeks went pink. 'Oh my god. You should ditch me in every plan.' Saying this, she suddenly hugged me, whispering, 'Thank you.'

It felt so good that I could feel like I was soaking in the air with my aura of bliss.

#2: Sacrifices

After a few days since that trek, we planned to go to a movie. I called her. 'Movie tonight!'

'Which one?'

'*Sonu ke titu ki sweety.*'

'Oh', she paused, and after a while, mumbled, 'okay.' be ready by 8.30 she said, Ok and hung up.

The movie was at 9. The others had already left, and I was waiting for her. We reached the movie a bit late also due to traffic and missed the first few minutes.

'We should have come early,' I sulked. 'We've missed most of it.'

'Not at all,' she said. 'The first few minutes are just Kartik Aaryan getting trolled by another character's family member for not believing in arranged marriages.'

I was confused. 'How did you know all this?'

'I watched the film yesterday,' she shrugged.

'What?' I was speechless.

'I came because you called,' she said, looking at me directly.

I started blushing hard, My love and respect for her only went higher.

'Aww,' I smiled and tapped her head with mine. 'This is the best thing anyone has ever said to me.'

'*Hange navvu* (We are like that).' She asked me to not tell the others to which I agreed, and we continued watching the movie.

For a second, I had a particularly brave idea. I wanted to hold her hand, but my heart was thumping harder at the thought of it. Disregarding it, I gathered courage even though my hands were still shaking. I brought my hand close to hers, keeping my fist open.

She got the hint. Soon, her hand was above mine. 'Why are you shivering?' she asked.

'It's nothing. I think I'm a bit cold.' I said but it was the nervousness

She offered me her jacket but I refused by saying now I will be ok I guess, while saying this I pointed out holding hands. to which she laughed and offered her jacket though I put it around my chest with my other hand keeping the holding hand still. and continued watching the movie.

#3: *Healthy flirting* (there's no such thing)

Varun, Alisha and I went to eat *pani puri* on High Street. She had already been flirting with me probably just for fun, but she would say things like 'I like you,' and I would just laugh it off. Because I really didn't know how else to react since it was the first time that a girl was flirting with me in the way she would. In fact, she wouldn't even be discreet about it. She would flirt in front of Varun, Nikil and all our other friends. Maybe if I had shown some courage and said 'I like you too,' this would be a totally different story. Sigh.

That day, even Varun teased us while we were having *pani puri*. There was some flirting happening when he warned us that eventually one or both of us will become serious. 'Be careful,' he winked. We laughed it off while he said, 'Only time will tell.'

It was all going well, but as time passed, I found myself becoming more and more attached to her. The situation seemed similar at her end, but she handled her emotions well, while I... well, you'll find out.

#4: *Dance*

I love to dance, usually flailing my arms wildly, but my shyness overtook me and prevented me from being able to move. I have always been a fan of good dance steps. But the way she danced was mesmerizing; I could keep looking at her without a single blink. She enjoys dancing, and the first time, my pub experience was 'LIIT' like our drinks and her dance. One hell of a combination it was. After seeing her dance for a while, I too felt like matching my steps with hers and kept trying to make her see me and call me over to the dance floor. 'Please look this way,' my mind begged.

It has always amazed me that whenever I utter something inwardly but from my heart, she happens to listen to it most of the time. The same happened here. She approached me and dragged me to the dance floor. I stood there, barely being able to move my arms, admiring her steps, when all of a sudden things around me started moving in slow motion. Maybe it was the combined effect of the alcohol and my exhilarated heart. Her grace and elegance took my love for her to a whole new high.

#5: C 102

After the first year, although things, in general, were normal, she was sick of staying in the hostel. She wanted to move out, but because of her parents, she couldn't. Meanwhile, Rohan who was in her class became friends and he wanted to move out from his hotel as well, but he was having trouble finding a roommate. I had known him since playing volleyball for the college team together, so one day we met in the cafeteria. They had already planned everything by then and pitched it so well that I had to say yes. And there my regular college life turned upside down. Our room was C102. Before moving in, I used to go to the gym in the morning and play volleyball in the evenings. But since we would sleep in the same room and I needed to wake up early for the gym, for which I had to set an alarm, it would irritate them. That was the end of my gym routine. Even with volleyball, I would play on alternate days to be able to spend more time with her. She was upset about it, but I had made my choice.

And as time passed, unknowingly, I developed deeper feelings for her. I could spend every day with her, every hour and every minute. Just by laying in our only big bean Bag and A box made a table which was basically a TV stand to keep our laptop on it and we used to watch movie after movie and lots of binge-watch of shows. Those were the good times.

#6 The Selflessness Act.

I was already in love, and I just needed the perfect moment to confess my feelings to her. For a shy guy like me, it was as difficult as climbing Mount Everest. One day, we went to Mumbai for a trip, and while street shopping, she wanted to eat cheesecake from one Leopold Café. I had her shopping bags in my hand, and a bit of cake fell on my shoe. Suddenly, she leaned in with the tissue in her hand. I was confused but teased her a bit. '*Arreh*, there's no need to clean at all!'

She laughed. 'You wish!' She grabbed a new tissue and went ahead to wipe the cake off my shoe.

I immediately stepped back, saying, 'Hey, are you crazy? I was only kidding!'

'What's the big deal?' she said casually.

'Nope, never do that again,' I said, and wrapped my arms around her, giving her a peck on her head. It was beyond me how, despite being so popular in college and usually donning a no-nonsense attitude all the time, she did not hesitate even for a second. Could you help fall for her deeper? She would do anything for the people she cared about and never miss a chance to show that. I was so proud of her. Whenever we used to fight, I found myself remembering these moments and crawled back to her and quickly apologised. She would take it so cutely.

They say love happens at a particular moment, but here in my case, there were several such beautiful events, and I am so glad to have experienced that beautiful phase multiple times. I could do this my whole life. (in Captain America styles)

In between those moments most of the college time has passed we left with hardly a few months and I had to lot to cover, like getting placed and winning her heart.

CHAPTER V

THE UNDERGROUND BAR

'*Kab hoga yaar tera* placement? I have been waiting for you to get placed. I will come from Belgavi to Pune for three to four days,' said Disha on call. She was my friend from engineering.

I was very frustrated because every one of my friends had gotten placed and were having the best days of their life, staying up late with no fear of attendance, no obligation to go to college, and instead of going for trips. There was no pressure left for them regarding the next step in their life; they could even grow a beard as they pleased! But I was completely screwed. I had to sleep early if I got shortlisted in companies, shave myself clean, wear the same white and black outfit and endure the arduous walk along the same ominous corridor again and again. I performed decently in clearing group discussions and interviews, but the aptitude test gave me nightmares.

After Disha said it like that, I felt a bit unsettled but wanted to reassure her – and myself. 'You come this weekend. I have given the two interviews today. *Kuch toh hoga iss bar* (Something will happen this time).'

'*Pakka? Avau kya?* (Sure? Should I come?)'

'See, there's just a month left to wind up the Pune thing, so yeah, come. *Jo hoga wo daekengae* (We'll see what happens).'

'Okay, *chalo* then, all the best. I really wish *ki tera hoga iss company mein* (I really wish you make it with this company).'

'I wish the same. But I am pretty sure I will. *Chalo*, bye-bye. Book your tickets so that you can arrive on Saturday morning.'

'*Aj toh* Monday *hai* (Today is Monday). I will book tomorrow or the day after.'

'Cool, no problem.' I replied, hung up and went back to my room, Alisha and Rohan were playing PUBG, so I joined them. After a few hours of playing, Rohan had a bus to catch, so he went to pack; he was going to Mumbai to meet his sister and told us he would return on Wednesday early morning at around 2. 'I will call you. Come to pick me up near Wakad Bridge.'

It was around 6 in the evening.

Alisha said, 'Karna, tea, please.' It was the only thing I was good at, so regardless of whether it was morning or evening, it was always my turn to make tea according to C 102 house rules.

I happily went to make tea; it would only be Alisha and me in the house for two days. As it was all coming to an end, I was sort of planning to confess to her about how I felt. While making tea, I was thinking about all the ways in which I could tell her. After a few minutes, she peeked into the kitchen. 'Do you need any help?'

'Yes, please. Wash the cups, *na*.' She started washing the cups when Rohan shouted from the bedroom, 'Alisha, your phone is ringing!'

'Who is it?'

'Ayan,' he said and brought the phone to the kitchen.

'My hands are wet. Answer it, and put it on speaker.' Rohan did as he was told.

'Hi, what's up?' the voice on the call said.

'Nothing really, just washing teacups. What's up with you?'

'I am in Pune, near the Mercedes showroom.'

Everyone was taken aback in their own way. She was pleasantly shocked, and Rohan was perplexedly surprised, as he was leaving. My surprise was more profound. 'Fuck my life,' I almost muttered under my breath. 'What timing, bro.' Just now I was so excited thinking about how the next two days would go, and all of a sudden my luck reversed as if in a parallel universe. How bad could these days go?

She was still on call. 'What are you doing here?'

'Came to see you. I had two days' leave. My boss had some function to attend, so I jumped in here. Come pick me up.'

'Okay, okay. I will see you in five minutes.' She hung up.

She looked at me with puppy eyes. 'Karna, please pick him up *na*. It will take time for me to get ready, and Rohan has a bus or I would have sent him.'

'Okay, sure,' I said, but I was not willing to although I had no choice. If I refused, she would be upset about it and keep asking why, to which I wouldn't have an answer.

It was about kilometres away, and I was thinking about why I did not ask about her and Ayan earlier. Till now, I had never had the guts to ask about whether they were dating or were just friends.

To others, it looked like they were dating, but I was not ready to accept it. But neither could I confront her. If she said yes, I would be forced to withdraw my feelings for her. And for that to happen, I would have to stay away from her completely. Just the thought of it terrified me.

While these thoughts ran across my mind, I reached the showroom where he was waiting. 'Hi,' I said. We didn't have much conversation while coming back, barely even small talk. When we reached home, Rohan had left already. It was only Alisha, Ayan and me all alone.

Both of them were busy talking to each other while sipping tea on the balcony. I was in my room thinking about how to pass the next days when she came to my room. 'Dinner outside?' she said.

'Cool. But Nikil is coming over. He just texted for me to pick him up, and I think he will stay here tonight.'

'Oh, okay. Then the four of us can go.'

I was trying my best to cancel the dinner plan, even if that meant resorting to lies, but she was not taking the hint. I tried further. 'He might take me to Desi Aroma for biryani. I told him about Ayan coming and that you guys might go out, so he made plans for the two of us.'

'I can tell you're lying to me,' she said quietly.

'Call him and ask. Why should I lie?' I knew she was not going to call him. I even gave her my phone with Nikil's number on the dial pad.

She finally acquiesced. 'Okay. I am not calling him, and you can go for now. But if this is a lie and I find that out later, then just remember that that moment onwards I won't even speak to you.'

'If I have lied *na*. Cool, I am not lying.'

I immediately left for the hostel. On the way, I called Nikil and explained to him the situation. He seemed down for playing along but on one condition: we were going to eat biryani at Desi Aroma and I would be paying. I agreed. 'Get ready in five. I am on the way.'

After we had dinner, I reminded him that he was to stay at our place.

'Anything, man. You just pay my biryani bill, that's all.'

He was always suspicious about the way I felt about Alisha. Whenever he asked if anything was going on between us, if I told him the truth, he would start teasing me. So I learnt to evade the topic entirely and would always dodge that question.

We went home, and as soon as we hit the bed, the biryani effect started to kick in. I was playing PUBG to get rid of the fatigue. He was not a fan, so he was playing Tetris instead. After a while, he dozed off. I was wondering whether to wait till they arrived or go to sleep when a text popped up on my phone. It was Alisha saying that his friends were coming over and that they might stay.

'Okay,' I texted back. 'I will be asleep, so the door will be locked, but you have the keys.'

'I know I have the keys,' she immediately responded. 'I texted you because I am sleeping in my place. Don't let Nikil sleep there in the other room since he and his friends will party.'

I typed 'Okay', hit 'Send' and turned to sleep.

When I woke up the next morning, she was there lying in her own space. I checked my phone. There was a text informing me that we will go out for lunch and will drink, so I was not to make other plans.

As soon as I saw the text, I knew I needed to scoot before she woke up. Nikil was up already. I told him we would go get breakfast near the college. After breakfast, we went to his room, as I had to escape the lunch plan. I stayed there playing FIFA. At some point, her call arrived. To placate her, I said, 'I will meet you. Just send me the location.'

After a few hours of playing, she called again. This time, her voice sounded angry.

'But I haven't received a text from you.' I opened WhatsApp; there was her text. 'I'm so sorry,' I urged. 'I will be there in ten.'

I reached the location when they were about to leave – just as planned. She was angry with me for sure, but if

I hadn't shown up, it would have been a totally different thing. Now that I was here though, I had some point of defence.

We sat for a while, I had a pint of beer and then we left for home. Ayan's friends also went on their way.

I was a bit scared, because she never lashed out in public, and it felt like a ticking bomb waiting to explode. Ayan went to the balcony for a smoke, and I went to my room. In no time, she barged in. And there was the blast that I had been dreading.

'Why are you behaving like this?' she demanded. 'You are avoiding us on purpose, I can see that.'

'No, please,' I tried to make my case. 'It was not intentional. I was playing FIFA with Nikil and some other guys. A tournament was going on, so I couldn't leave in the middle.' For this, I received several more words of rebuke.

At last, she said, 'You said Disha might come this weekend or the next, right?'

I nodded. She replied, 'If you miss tonight's plan, I will stay in the hostel when she comes and won't meet her or you.'

I had no choice left there. 'I will come,' I sighed. 'Where are we going?'

'The Underground Bar. Sherya and her boyfriend are also coming.'

All I wanted was to cancel the plan. I would only be third-wheeling between Alisha and Ayan and the other couple. But I didn't dare refuse since she had already given me her warning about Disha. It would be worse because Ayan and I didn't talk much. I used to just reply to whatever he asked, and it was one-way traffic. Just because of her, to ensure that she didn't get upset over it, I used to talk in bits and pieces. The more I stayed away from him though, the better it was for me.

At around 8, Sherya called and asked us to come down, as they were waiting at the gate. The three of us met them promptly. It was about twenty minutes' ride to the Underground Bar.

True to its name, the place was lit like a tunnel. I was almost feeling anxious and claustrophobic given how dark and confined the space was. We ordered a bucket of beer. Sherya and I were merely acquaintances; it was only because of Alisha that I met them. I am not good with new people, so I had only Alisha and Sherya left to talk to.

After a couple of beers, they started dancing; Alisha and Sherya both loved to dance. We boys were sitting at the table letting the alcohol kick in. I usually find the courage to dance after two or three pints, but that day, I was not willing to dance at all, and so I just kept drinking. It was the second mistake of the day; the first one was coming here at all. I should have danced, because it makes me sick watching Alisha and Ayan dance together. Moreover, I was upset about the placement thing; everyone here was placed, and I was left in the bottom 100 among 750 students.

When she called me to join them, I refused, but then Sherya also tried to pull me to the dance floor. 'I am not in the mood, please leave me be,' I protested, but Sherya had guessed why I was not in the mood; she knew I liked Alisha. She said, 'I know how you are feeling. I have been there in your place. Don't worry, it will pass.'

I was caught off-guard. 'What? How could you notice? We don't even know each other very well... But you are right, yeah, it feels terrible.'

My feelings for Alisha were unknown to everyone except Rohan, and here I could have said something like 'No, you are wrong' and diverted the topic to placements.

But being intoxicated, or perhaps after seeing them dance, I felt like I needed someone to talk to. She said the right words at the wrong time, and that response was my third mistake of the day. After our talk, I saw Sherya whispering something to Alisha, after which the latter approached me.

'Karna, what happened? Why are you so dull today? Come, we will dance.'

'Nah,' I said. 'I am okay.'

'If you're okay, then come dance,' and she pulled me to the dance floor. I stayed there for a while, clapping and moving my legs awkwardly with a forced smile plastered on my face. I wanted to slide away from there as smoothly as possible. Alisha noticed and asked where I was headed. I pointed to my phone. 'I'm getting a call, will be back in two minutes.' She gave me a thumbs-up, and I went outside,

I sat near the *paan* shop beside the pub and felt like I could use a smoke. Up until then, I had never felt the urge to smoke all by myself. I took one cigarette and was contemplating lighting it and looking for a matchbox when Alisha's call arrived.

'Where are you? Come inside!'

'I will be there in two.' No sooner had I said it than she was already outside and walking towards me. I chucked the cigarette away before she could notice.

'Oh man, it's so cool and fresh outside. We will stay here for a while.' She began browsing through her Insta. I spoke in a very low, hesitant voice.

'*Oye*, are you guys committed? You and Ayan...'

'It's nothing of that sort. He likes me, and I like him too. That's it really.'

It was confusing. 'Oookkkaayyyyy...'

'Did you say something to Sherya?'

At that moment, I knew I was screwed, and it was time to pay for slipping earlier. I was scared.

'I don't remember exactly,' I muttered. 'She asked me something, and I didn't completely understand it and said something else, after which she left.'

'Okay, but... Anyway, come now, let's go inside. We will talk again at home.'

I knew I had fucked it up.

We went inside, had food, along with the warm beer left in bottles, and headed back home. They were planning for an afterparty, and Ayan asked me about the half-full bottle of Dewar's at my place. 'Yeah,' I said. 'If you guys want it, you can have it. I am done for the day.'

Alisha nodded, 'Same.'

Sherya's boyfriend had to wake up early for his job, so the plan ultimately got cancelled. They dropped us where they had picked us from and went home themselves.

Now I had to escape from the scene, so I turned to Alisha. 'Sai had called me to his flat to play FIFA. Nikil is also there, so I am going. It will be late by the time I'm done, so I will crash at his place.'

'No, you are not going anywhere. We need to talk.'

'About what?'

'Come upstairs. We will go inside and talk.'

She was angry and upset when we entered the flat. Ayan went to the balcony to smoke while we went to my room.

'Karna, what did you tell her?' she demanded.

'Nothing at all,' I shrugged. 'I already told you, I don't remember exactly what happened.'

'Then why would she say stuff like I am playing with your feelings. She asked me to talk to you and set things straight because you're in a bad state.'

I started laughing. 'Oh, that? It's nothing, really. It was about the girl I had proposed to and who said I was her best friend. I was wondering whether to call and wish her; it is her birthday. Then Sherya appeared and said something. I was not even listening to her when she asked something and mumbled something incoherent.'

'What?' Alisha frowned in confusion.

'Yeah, total misunderstanding.'

'Okay, I believe you, but still, is there anything you want to tell me?'

'Nope, there's nothing.'

She left to remove her makeup, seeming a bit unconvinced. Although I lied, it was enough to stave off the confrontation for the moment. And now I had to make a call to Sherya and give her an update about it. I unlocked my phone to text her when Alisha reappeared.

'Karna, do you like me? Tell me the truth? Don't lie.'

I stood quietly for a few seconds and then slowly went near her. I looked into her eye; I was so close that I could feel her breath. 'Yes.'

I leaned a bit forward, and she reciprocated. We both kissed. At that moment, Ayan came in and saw us.

Sigh. If only life was that filmy and unrealistic.

'No,' I said. 'Why would you think that?'

'It's nothing,' she said absentmindedly. 'I was just confirming.' Then she continued with her makeup removing process.

I was relieved. Sherya's reply arrived. 'Okay.'

Ayan was to leave the next day. By the time I woke up, it was already 11, and Ayan was gone. Things were back to normal.

Well, at least that's what I believed and let her believe

CHAPTER VI

THE RIVERSIDE VILLA

Things were back to normal. Like old times, the three of us were sitting in the same room and chilling, playing PUBG, scrolling through Instagram and streaming songs and movies. It was almost 7 in the evening, and we had just had coffee. Suddenly, an email notification from the placement committee popped up. With my heart in my mouth, I opened it immediately. The wait was over. I had gotten placed.

It was probably one of the happiest days of my life. I showed the mail to Alisha. She screamed in her excitement and gave me a tight hug. Rohan was happy too. Many parties and night-out plans had been cancelled just because of my placement or the lack thereof. The next best thing was that I could finally grow a beard and say goodbye to those bloodsucking white formals and that nerve-wracking placement committee. Alisha quickly dropped a text in the group chat. Messages of congratulations were pouring in from all around. The one sad part was that it was a 'dry day', and there was no booze to make the day absolutely perfect.

The doorbell rang, and Rohan opened the door. It was the whole gang – Madhu, Varun and Nikil. We were all overjoyed. Now the entire squad had been placed. All that was left was to party, go on trips and make the most of our time left. The road ahead had endless possibilities.

Madhu produced a half-filled McDowell's. It had been arranged by a friend just to celebrate my achievement. Nikil held my hand while Madhu opened the bottle and poured the contents down my mouth. No mixing. Completely raw.

I had never drunk raw whiskey until then, but I couldn't care less. That evening, I was going to brave it all. I had to drink the whole thing in a single, long gulp with a break of hardly ten seconds. I felt nothing for a while.

Soon, everyone had proceeded into my room. Songs started playing, and the disco lights were on. Everyone was dancing, and the alcohol slowly started kicking in. But I had already started moving my body to the music. It was that day that I realised that it's not always intoxication that makes you let yourself go; sometimes, the energy comes from within you, your mental state. I was in a cocoon of bliss that evening, seeing everyone around enjoying themselves so much.

Phantoms & Friends by Old Man Canyon was playing, and in front of me I could picture me and my friends, in a sunroof car, with bottles of chilled beer around us, our hair ruffled by the evening breeze, our faces lit with the golden hues of the setting sun. In that moment, we were oblivious of all the pains and troubles of the world.

My phone cruelly rang and broke my reverie. It was Disha. I ran to the balcony for some quiet, answered the phone and screamed, 'I got placed!'

'What?! When? Which company? Congratulations!!!' her voice rose.

'I found out only a while ago. Book your tickets ASAP. I'll tell you everything once you're here.'

'This is what I'd called you about. I just booked my tickets. I will be there on Friday morning. See how lucky I am for you. I decide to come this weekend and book tickets, and you get placed.'

'So it appears,' I laughed. 'Thank you for being my lucky charm.'

'Don't thank me. Give me one hell of a party instead. It has been ages since my last drink.'

'Sure, I'll take care of that. You just come here, I will make sure it's the best, most memorable weekend!'

'We'll see! Now go and enjoy the party. I will call later. Congratulations again.'

Later, after they had gotten tired and went back to their places, I informed Alisha and Rohan that Disha was coming on Friday morning and that we would need to plan something. They readily agreed. We started to make a list. Initially, we were considering Goa or Mumbai for two or three days but then ended up booking a villa, with a pool no less, in Lonavala. It was mostly Alisha's idea. Rohan was to take care of the booking. I was in charge of arranging for people and car. Prajwal had a car, and he would be in for sure. We asked Madhu, Varun and Nikil. Varun had some work about the project report, so he refused, but the others were ready. Sai too had no option but to give in, because Disha would kill him if he cancelled on her. Snehal was in her hometown.

So it was me, Alisha, Rohan, Prajwal, Nikil, Madhu, Sai and Disha. The villa we decided upon was called The Riverside Villa.

It was finally Friday morning. She was supposed to arrive at 6, but she came earlier, at 5, when I was still sleeping. When I woke up, to my utter shock, there were ten missed calls. Poor Disha had been waiting in the cold and dark for thirty minutes. I frantically called her to apologize. She was surprisingly calm. 'Come *aaramse*,don't rush.'

Thankfully, the highway was devoid of traffic, and I reached in five minutes. Seeing her waiting under Wakad

Bridge made me feel guiltier. I quickly got down from my bike and hugged her. I kept apologising until she was visibly irritated. 'Can you stop, please?' she slapped my arm. I apologised again for apologising. This made her face break into a helpless chuckle.

'Welcome to Pune,' I said.

'Thank you. Now please can we get going?'

'We will, but you must be hungry. Would you like to get Maggie or something to drink, coffee or tea? A bike ride with tea early in the morning feels amazing. What do you think?'

'I know you want to drink more than me. Why not? Let's start with tea and the bike ride.'

We went up to the college, where Kailasha Anna was. 'Two special ginger tea.' He smiled and nodded. Our insides needed that soothing warmth in the chilly morning.

Afterwards, we went home. The rest were sleeping; she too wanted to sleep for a bit, and so did I. But I couldn't sleep, so I got up and made coffee while listening to music. I sipped the coffee on the balcony, where the sun was all set to rise. I was on my beanbag, taking in the fresh morning air, on the top floor, with half of the drowsy city stretching out in front of me. It was a good start to the day. I dropped a text on the group chat, asking everyone to be there by 11 so that we could have lunch at Lonavala and reach the resort by 2.

After some time, Rohan woke up. We were bored, so we tried playfully annoying Alisha while she tried to maintain her sleep. It was like playing with fire, but it was fun. She was about to wake up, so I went to the kitchen and made coffee. 'Come on, we have coffee. Wake up before it gets cold, sleepyhead.' I knew it would make her rise from the bed. It worked of course. Like a child, she got up and, rubbing her eyes, said, 'Thank you...' I decided that if I were rewarded with this cuteness every morning, I would make her coffee for a lifetime.

After a while, Disha woke up too, and I introduced her to both. She knew about them already; they had talked on the phone earlier. Meanwhile, I ordered food from Anna Idli. Disha tried my coffee and complimented me; it felt nice, and I basked in my temporary glory.

'I'm the one who taught him,' Alisha winked at Disha, who promptly took her side, teasing me together with her. For them, it was a bonding moment. Soon, Prajwal, Madhu and Nikil arrived. Disha didn't have any trouble getting along with my friends; she was a total people-person.

Apart from Madhu and Nikil, who had already eaten, everyone had the idlis. After some time, we left for the resort. We had only one car and too many people, so Nikil and I decided that we would go by bike. Sai said he would join later and also come by bike as it was just sixty kilometres away. After we were done taking photos together, we were finally ready to embark on the trip.

The rest of them reached before Nikil and me, and we met them at the hotel. They were all purposefully teasing me since Disha was there. But it was all in good humour. Lunch was filled with laughter and happiness in the air. All of a sudden, I received a text from an unknown number.

'Hi bro,' it said, 'it's Ayan. Do you mind if come?'

I thought he was referring to C 102. 'Not at all, bro. Sure.'

'Thanks, man,' the reply arrived instantly. 'But don't tell her.'

I was fine with all that – until I realised how dumb I was. It was Rohan who pointed it out. '*Bhai*,' he texted,'did you just agree to Ayan joining us?'

Fuck my life. I explained to him what had happened. Rohan asked me to text him and let him know that some of us were not comfortable with him, so could he join us the next time. To me, this was an impossible task since it felt rude, so I decided to let him meet us at the resort. I could have said all this to Alisha, but for some unknown reason, I refrained from doing so.

As soon as we spotted the pool, all of us immediately got busy with changing our clothes. In no time, we were jumping into the pool. Nikil was acting as DJ, so he remained dry. I was walking under the water since I didn't know how to swim, but Alisha was helping me discover my skills. I could have been floating like the rest, but the pool was at five feet and I was at six feet two inches. She eventually gave up on me. After some time, Sai arrived and immediately removed his T-shirt, handed the phone to Nikil and jumped into the water. After they took a few pictures, I came out of the pool as I was shivering, took a bath in hot water and joined Nikil in his DJing endeavour. While the girls left to wash up, the boys hung around by the pool, smoking.

An unknown number was calling me. Ayan. 'Bro, come pick me up.'

'Yeah, of course, bro. Send me your location.

Nobody knew yet that he would be arriving. This is when I told them, narrating the entire scenario. Everyone was pissed at me, tsk-tsking at my 'utter dumbness'. Little did they know that I was more upset and angry than any of them. But I was helpless. 'Please,' I urged. 'Cooperate. Don't be rude to him.' If they were rude to him, he would be offended, and his taking offence would upset Alisha, which would make me sad. I left to pick him up.

As soon as we arrived back at the villa, he asked for her. 'Probably taking a bath,' I answered. He said hi to everyone, and they responded casually, which was frankly quite relieving for me. As she was upstairs, he waited in the hall watching TV. I was introducing Disha to him when I heard Alisha's gasp. 'What the... What are you doing?'

Ayan shrugged. 'Felt like joining you guys. Asked Karna. He was cool, so I came.'

The expression of shock still hadn't left Alisha's face. It was like she was tired of his unannounced appearances. Whatever she was feeling, she managed to control it. She took him upstairs while Disha dragged me to the room.

'Why the fuck is he here? And you let him join? Are you mad?'

I explained everything to her just like I had done before with the boys.

'God!' she threw her arms in exasperation. 'Learn to say no to the things you don't like before it's too late.'

'Yeah,' I slouched against the wall. 'I should... but it's difficult me for me, because I keep thinking that a no would hurt the other person. And... I can't handle that. It's me that gets hurt. I feel it's better for me this way.'

'*Arrey bhai*! In which year are you living? The 1900s? The world has changed, Karna. Get your mind straight.'

Silently, I sat on the bed, my shoulders drooping. She came and sat beside me, patting my hand. 'Anyway, he has arrived now, so there's nothing we can do about it. Now try not to spoil this time for yourself. Be normal, and don't think about it much. We will talk about it later.'

I heaved a big sigh, preparing myself to act normal.

At around 7 in the evening, in the hall, there was loud music playing with people swaying to the beat. Sai and Disha were matching steps and apparently having a great time. Madhu paused the music.

'Alright, people, let's get this party started. One by one, each of you will tell me what you want to have tonight so that we can get drunk out of our minds. Who do we have for whiskey?'

Prajwal, Sai, Nikil, Rohan and Ayan raised their hands. Alisha, Disha and I were up for a beer.

'*Macha*, get one pack of smoke extra,' Prajwal said.

'I was about to ask,' Madhu replied.

'I knew it, bro, that's why we are brothers,' Prajwal winked.

Everyone in the room started guffawing and cheering. 'Woohoooo... we've got some bromance here...'

Madhu, Prajwal and Nikil went to get us booze and food. Disha, Sai and I came out and sat on the edge of the pool with our feet in the water. We talked about our engineering days when life seemed so much simpler. 'Now it is all about job, money, marriage and so on,' said Disha.

Sai and I knew about her family problems, so we wanted to distract her. Sai ignited the cigarette and passed it to me. The cigarette was being passed around between us when Rohan arrived and took his seat beside me. I turned around to check what Alisha and Ayan were doing. The door was open, and there she was, lying on the sofa while he was giving her a head massage. I felt sick.

I could not think about anything else, so I pretended that I had gotten a text from Prajwal. 'Guys, Prajwal says they need cash to buy smoke. The seller isn't accepting GPay or Paytm.'

I took my bike and headed out, and called Prajwal and asked where they were. He sent me his location, which I could cover in ten minutes. When I met them, they were waiting for food.

'What's up, man?' Madhu asked. 'What are you doing here?'

'Nothing, bro. I just needed to clear my mind.'

'Why, what happened?'

'Ayan, man.'

'Karna, you dumb asshole. Why did you even agree for him to join?'

'It's all a misunderstanding, Madhu, or he wouldn't be here.'

I explained the circumstances to them again. Even though they totally understood, Madhu and Prajwal couldn't help shaking their heads. 'Man,' Madhu clicked his tongue, 'I have friends in my circle closer to me than he is to you. But I never crash their party like this. He fucking spoiled everyone's mood. You just wait. I'll make jokes and ensure that he regrets coming here.'

Prajwal and Nikil nodded their assent. 'Same, let's do this.'

'Please, guys, let's not. It will spoil everyone's mood, especially Alisha's, and you know how that would affect me. Plus, Disha is here for a short while. Let these days be memorable for her in a good way. You guys can scold me or do whatever you want later, but just... let's treat him better, even if it's with a fake smile and small talk.'

Everyone seemed convinced for now, but I didn't know how they would react, especially Madhu.

Once we reached the villa, the place had been set for playing poker, with chips divided for each person and kept aside. Everyone rushed to get their preferred seats. Madhu started making drinks. I was with my regular chilled beer. The game was going well till people started being butterfingered and spilling their drinks on the cards.

Disha and Alisha wanted to dance, so Nikil volunteered to be DJ. I lay on the couch admiring their dance moves while Sai also joined them. It really felt like a party whose memories I wanted to keep recorded in my mind forever. Everyone seemed happy.

Later, Madhu and Prajwal went to the poolside to lure those who were staying next to our villa with the expensive scotch that Madhu had brought. Meanwhile, both girls had gotten tired, and Sai had retreated to his own space with smoke and lightly tapping his feet to the rhythm of the songs. Alisha went and sat on the couch next to Ayan. Whenever I saw her with him, my chest would feel heavy with apprehension, and there was this profound sadness that I cannot quite articulate. At the time, I didn't know when I would ever get over it.

I went outside and joined Disha. Madhu and Prajwal had worked out something with those girls whom they were trying to tempt because they were now drinking together. I thought it was the expensive drinks that did the trick, but it turned out that they had more pricey stuff. But fortunately, they needed some cigarettes, and Prajwal always had the stock. They soon introduced them to us. After some time, the whole girl squad arrived, and outside it was more of a party scene than the inside, so everyone came out with their drinks. With the Marshall speaker blasting, everyone was on their feet, having the time of their lives as if there was nothing to worry about – except me.

When the girls went back to their villa, all of us could see the disappointment in Madhu and Prajwal's faces, because to them it felt like despite their best efforts, they were unable to give their moments some closure.

For the first time, Ayan joined Madhu and Prajwal fighting for cigarettes, while Disha, Alisha, Rohan and I were sitting a bit away from them talking about old times. Alisha was narrating our C 102 quest to Disha. It was the only time I was spending with Alisha without him being present. As it was getting late, one by one they were all going inside to have some food and call it a night.

As Prajwal, Nikil, Sai, Disha and I were still up, we needed a bonfire since it was quite uncomfortably chilly. It was too late to ask the manager, so we decided to join the security guard's little campfire sort of thing. With our hands getting warmer, our conversations flowed more easily. Everyone was sharing their deepest secrets, including their crushes, first times and life goals. If someone had a guitar, it would have made for the cherry on top. It was almost 4 in the morning when we decided to get some sleep and retreat to our rooms. Before that, however, we wanted to smoke up, and that's what we did.

'Bro, I think you are making a mistake,' Sai said after a puff.

'What mistake?' I looked around uneasily.

'This thing between you and Alisha... better to clear it as soon as possible. If you don't, from what I have known of you in all this time, I can say that you will find yourself in big trouble.'

Disha nodded. '*Haan*, you are so sentimental, so emotional. Later on, don't call me and cry like a baby. There's still time. Talk to her and tell her how you feel about her.'

I smoked while trying to form a response. 'This did cross my mind, so when we went to that Underground Pub, I asked her if she and Ayan are in a relationship. She said they aren't and that they're just friends. "He likes me, and so do I," something like that. I don't know whether it's true, but it was all I wanted to hear, so I didn't ask for any further details.

'If she says this, it's fine, but still, it's better to clear it out as soon as possible. I don't want you to suffer,' Disha said while Sai nodded.

'I know, but let's see. I will try to sort it out soon. Thanks for the advice. It means a lot coming from you guys.'

By this time, the first rays of the day were already peeking from the clouds. We went to sleep at around 6 in the morning and woke up at 10 with the receptionist's call, which was a reminder about our checkout at 11. We hurriedly freshened up and soon left the villa, dropping Ayan near the bus stop. 'Thanks, man,' he said, 'for letting me join you guys. I had a wonderful evening.' His bus was already waiting. In no time and after this our paths never crossed each other.

we had left Lonavala far behind with memories indelible in our hearts and minds, and then some...

CHAPTER VII

THE DINNER DATE

Disha was all set to go back the next day, and before that, we wanted to have a house party, the proper one, with in-house cooking. This wasn't a problem, because Prajwal and Disha were damn good in the kitchen. Prajwal decided to do the prawn fry and Disha, chicken biryani. Rohan and I had to get the groceries. We went early in the morning and picked up all the items on the list. Prajwal would be buying the prawns.

As Disha's bus was at 9 in the evening, we had planned for lunch instead of dinner. Sai went back to his flat, saying that he would see us at night to see Disha off. Nikil wasnot in the mood to stay either because of non-vegetarian food being cooked. Since I would not eat the chicken, I asked him to get vegetarian Hyderabadi biryani from Aroma House. That convinced him, and he finally agreed to come.

Remember the feeling when you go back home from the hostel and all your relatives arrive to meet and greet you? The hustle and bustle of scurrying feet, the laughter, the mood of festivity... That afternoon, the air in C 102 was very similar. Prajwal and Disha were in the kitchen with Alisha trying to help them. Rohan and I were only hanging out here and there, pretending to be busy with some work or the other, because if Alisha caught us with our real preoccupation, PUBG, we would be in grave danger.

After some time, lunch was ready. Nikil had also arrived by then. We had great food and the best company, and the room echoed with the sound of our laughter. Instead of asking them to pose, I took a picture of them as they were, unguarded, natural, oblivious of everything but the present moment. It was what kids nowadays call a 'candid capture'.

Like everything good, this time too came to an end. After finishing lunch, Prajwal, Nikil and I went to the balcony to smoke while the others stayed in the room playing PUBG. Disha joined us, and we talked about the trip took some pics there and Disha said,

'Thank you, guys, for everything. It was a much-needed break for me.'

'The pleasure is ours, Disha,' Prajwal said. 'You are a fun person to be around. I have never become this great friends with anyone within such a short time. So thank *you* for coming. Alisha's got her birthday soon. It will also be our last weekend in Pune. You must join us then.'

'Sure, I will definitely try to come.'

After we had tea in the evening, Nikil went back to the hostel. Disha started packing, and Prajwal decided that he would be going to his house after dropping Disha at the bus station since it was on the way.

It was almost 8 when Disha was saying her goodbyes to Rohan and Alisha. I picked up my helmet. 'Wait, you are also coming?' she seemed surprised.

'Of course. How did you even think that I would not come, *pagal*!' I poked her on the side of her head. That seemed to cheer her up. I placed her bag inside Prajwal's car while she sat in the front passenger seat. 'Bye, bro,' Prajwal said and immediately got confused. 'Macha, you are also coming?'

'Yeah, bro…'

'But why are you taking your bike? Come in the car with us.'

'You'd have to come back this way again, so I thought it's better with the bike.'

'Bro, seriously. You're insulting me, man, Come on, don't act smart. Just get in the car. I will drop you back here.'

'*Macha*, I was waiting for you to say this,' I teased.

Our banter continued in the car as we reached the pickup point. Sai was already waiting there; for the first time, he was on time, which took us by surprise.

The bus was also on time, and Disha became a bit teary-eyed but fought to hold herself back. 'Thank you,' she hugged me. I believe it was the first hug she had ever given me. I suddenly realised how important this trip must have been to her, and it pleased me to think that she was satisfied with her time with us.

'*Chalo* then, bye,' she said, turning away.

'Try to come next weekend if possible.'

'Sure. Alisha's birthday, no? I remember. I will try to come.'

We said bye for one last time.

After that, Sai went back to his flat, and Prajwal dropped me at C 102.

Rohan answered the door. He was on a call. 'Where's Alisha?' I mouthed the words. He pointed to our room.

On my way to the room, it felt so strange. All I could hear was the sound of my footsteps. Only a few hours ago, it was just the opposite. I thought of all the times I would go back to the hostel one day before the college started when no one would be there yet. School memories rushed in, which I did not particularly cherish. To avoid myself from heading into that zone, I went in and started talking to Alisha, who seemed tight-lipped, giving monosyllabic answers. Her behaviour confused me, so to cheer her up, I decided to show her the photos and dance videos I had taken of the past two days. She got up rather harshly, kept her phone aside and snatched my phone from my hand to look at the files in the gallery.

This did nothing to ease my confusion. Rohan entered the room. 'What's going on?'

'We are just looking at the photos of Lonavala.'

When he sat with us, I asked him with my expressions and hand gestures if Alisha was angry with me. He nodded, smiling. I began thinking about what could have gone wrong. She was swiping through the photos so fast that she could not have been looking at them clearly. She reached a dance video where it was just her and Disha dancing. This seemed to have held her attention for a while, and her mood was slightly turning back to normal.

But suddenly, her face became dark again. I realised that I had only focused the camera on Disha, and Alisha was not fully in the frame. That pissed her off. She locked my phone and threw it sideways where I was sitting. When I asked what had happened, she didn't answer. So I repeated. 'What happened? What did I do wrong?'

'She is a bit mad at you,' Rohan said, 'because you apparently ignored her in Lonavala. You didn't even speak with her.'

'And a bit more now!' she shouted. 'I fucking hate him more. Just look at the videos and photos. It's just Disha everywhere. It's like I don't even matter to him anymore!'

'Alisha... first of all, I am sorry if you felt like I was ignoring you. I wasn't. And secondly, Disha had no one close to her except me, so I had to be with her most of the time. That was the only reason why she's in most photos. There's nothing else here. I haven't ignored you at all.'

She seemed mad enough to not respond to my explanation. So I tried again. 'I am truly sorry. And also, you had someone to take care of you there. Maybe that's the reason I just took it lightly, I guess. It never occurred to me that you could be feeling something else. I should not have let this happen. I am so sorry, Alisha.'

Despite my pleading, she did not seem convinced. I went downstairs and got her some chocolate. Thrusting one chocolate in her hand, I said, 'Sorry, I will never ever make you feel like that again no matter who is there to take care of you.' I handed her one more chocolate. 'Sorry, again.'

By now, there was a hint of a smile on her angry face, which she was trying to hide. I knew one more chocolate would do the trick. I had three more chocolates with me, so I started giving them to her one by one, each time apologising. just like the first time after the trek, this trick always comes to rescue.

'Karna!' she finally said. 'Stop it now. You had me convinced at the third chocolate.' She hugged me and said, 'I know you had to be with her, but it's just that I hate it when you are with another girl. It makes me feel differently. I took it lightly because she was Disha. If it was someone else, I might have shouted at you there itself. But it's all good now. We are good. But I still hate you for that video.'

'I deserve that, I guess. I am sorry.'

'Can I get one chocolate for myself?' Rohan called with a grin.

'Bhai, you should also give her chocolates. You could have told me about this there itself. Because of this, I will be adding half the amount to Splitwise in your name.'

Alisha started laughing followed by Rohan.

Later that night, when Rohan was on the balcony attending a call, I suddenly thought of how Alisha and I hadn't had dinner together, just the two of us. I began daydreaming about it, imagining us in a rooftop restaurant with cool winds and romantic music surrounding us.

'Alisha', I began softly, 'next week will be our last one together in Pune. I was just thinking that we haven't had dinner together in all these two years. So how about we both go out for dinner as...a date?

'Just us two? What about Rohan?'

'I will talk to him, he should be cool with this.'

'If you can manage that, cool, we'll go after the last exam...on Friday, I guess?'

'It's on, then. Friday it is.'

The day before the dinner was to happen, I was full of restless anticipation regarding how the next night would go. I was even considering confessing my feelings for her. It was the only thing running in my mind even though I was preparing for the exam. Every few minutes, my mind wandered from the pages of the notes to my mental picture of our date, me saying the right words to her and the rest of the night going just as I'd like it to. Should I just blurt it out directly, I kept thinking, or is it better to go with the flow, dropping hints now and then until the final showdown?

Although I knew I had to focus on my exam preparation, I suddenly panicked thinking of the possibility that the restaurant could be fully booked, especially given that we would be going on a Friday evening. I quickly opened Zomato to book a table for two at Marine Drive, a famous rooftop restaurant that Varun had once mentioned for its ambience and live music. The rooftop was also supposed to have a garden with exotic plants and a huge fountain at the centre. It was just the perfect place for the date.

The exam was to be held in the afternoon. In C 102, I woke up at around 6 and started studying. I preferred studying early in the morning, unlike my roommates, and

I prepared till 9, after which I took a bath. At around 10, I woke them up and made tea for us. They weren't fully up until they had had the hot tea.

Alisha kept the teacup aside and gave me a hug, which seemed to have become our morning ritual. It was just the right start to the day. After tea, I went to the hostel and reached the lobby waiting for the lift. Varun appeared from the mess just when the lift door opened. We talked about my story and other concerns about our future.

After the last exam, when we met at the chai point, everyone started discussing evening plans. Some of them were interested in going to the KP side, and Varun, Prajwal and Nikil were okay with tagging along.

I was too scared to inform them that Alisha and I were going out. There was the chance that they would make a fuss out of it, which might offend her. I looked at her, hoping to be able to convey some sign for her to say no to this plan. But she didn't understand me, and when Madhu asked, she said, 'Yeah, I am in.' He was about to ask me but then said, 'If Alisha is coming, you will be coming for sure.' Within no time, everyone was on board and dispersed from that place.

I was so gutted and was in no mood to go to the KP side, but more than that, I kept feeling that she could have completely forgotten about it. If she remembered, she might have at least tried to bail herself out of that plan. I could have been wrong here, so to clarify, I decided to confront her while going back to C 102. 'Alisha, do you remember that we planned for dinner tonight?'

'Yes, of course, I remember. But all of us will be going out for one last time, and I want to be with all of them tonight, so I said yes to Madhu.'

This made me angry. She could have told me about it before I asked her; it would have made sense then. 'Oh, really?'

She sensed my disappointment and anger and started to try to console me. But I wasn't in the mood to hear anything. While this conversation was going on, some guy took a right turn in front of my bike. He was towards my left without any indicator, so I angrily shouted at him. She stopped talking, and I realised that I wasn't in my senses since this was the first time that I had ever shouted at an unknown person, that too in the middle of traffic with people around. Maybe the highest point of my temper had been reached that day.

At home, I apologised to her. 'I am sorry about that traffic incident. You must have been shocked since you haven't said anything in a while.'

'I haven't seen you in that way before.'

I decided to freshen up before we could talk further, so I took a bath, which helped me calm down. Rohan also came back. 'How was your exam?' 'The usual, okayish.'

He began chatting about his plans of the day; he would be going with his Chhattisgarh friends. 'What about you? Where are you both going?'

'To the KP side with the Karnataka gang.

'What about your dinner plans?' I had informed him about my plan earlier, according to which he made plans with his other friends.

'Change of plans.'

'When are you going to ask her, bro?'

'Certainly not today, but maybe on her birthday, which is like four days away.'

Alisha entered with three cups of tea on a plate. Rohan and I were surprised since she never made tea for even herself, and now she had made it for all of us.

'The queen self-serving tea,' Rohan teased. 'Let me get a pen to note the date down.' 'Shut up! I was only making it for Karna, and there was one cup extra, so I brought it for you too.' She

shrugged.

She kept the plate on the table and turned to face me. 'I know you wanted to go out with me. But it's our last day with all of them. Varun and Madhu are leaving tomorrow. We can go out some other day since we will be here till my birthday. Cheer up now. See, I have made tea. Drink up before it gets cold.'

It made sense, and the way she said it, with her soft voice, anyone would have been convinced. Plus, I was already floored with the fact that she had made tea. So I decided to cut her some slack and smiled. 'Sorry that you had to see my temper.'

'Not at all! I feel proud that I could see you in that avatar.'

Yet again, our fight ended with fun banter.

After some time, we got ready to meet the others. We booked a cab to Lord of the Drinks and picked up Prajwal on the way. What followed was a truly memorable day.

CHAPTER VIII

THE FINAL SURPRISE

The Beginning

There was one day to go for her birthday. I wanted to make it incredibly special, so I prepared pre-birthday gifts for her. While she was sleeping, I got her two T-shirts from H&M. Initially I had gone alone, but I had to return since all the options were confusing me. The second time, I took Snehal along. She was her roommate and was staying in the hostel.

Coming back, I placed the T-shirts next to her along with a note, wishing her an advanced birthday, along with a bouquet and chocolates. I made sure to take a picture of the whole thing.

Then Rohan went to get some stuff to decorate the room. Since she had no clue, and we had planned a surprise, we had to be discreet. Plus, we had very little time, so we had split the work. While Rohan was away, I went to the photo studio to collect some photos that I had planned to get printed in Polaroid-style, with space at the bottom for us to scribble the photo descriptions. We had also gotten a large mosaic photo for her wall.

While I was in the photo studio, my phone rang. It was her. 'Hello!' I answered excitedly.

'Karna!' she squealed. 'Thank you, thank you! When did you plan all of this? This was a total surprise. I was expecting gifts for my birthday, but these pre-birthday gestures... are so cute. Thank you.'

She said all of this at a stretch as the smile on my face kept widening listening to her excited voice. It drove me crazy just thinking of how adorable she could be. I was at the point in our dynamics where making her happy made me happier, and if she was sad, I would do anything in my power to bring a smile on her angelic face again.

'Where are you both?' she finally asked.

'We are near the college to have breakfast. I'm hoping to return by 10.' I called Rohan and told him that we needed to go back. 'Are you done with shopping?'

'Yeah, almost,' he said.

'Good. Be in the building parking lot. I will wait there.'

When I reached, Prajwal's car was there in the parking area. I texted him. 'Macha, come to the balcony and give me your car keys. Don't let her know.'

While dropping the keys, he gestured with his hands to ask why. I showed him the bags, and he gave a thumbs-up. Rohan arrived on time just as I was putting the stuff in the car. After placing all of the things safely, we both went up. As I was excited to see her reaction, I went straight to the room that she was in. She was lying in bed and got up as soon as she saw us. 'Madam,' Rohan asked, 'how was the surprise?' She hugged him, all the time saying thank you to us. 'Don't thank me, it was all Karna!'

'I know only Karna can give me a surprise like this.' She wrapped her arms around me and held them there for a while. 'Thank you again. Gift me like this on every birthday, okay?' She winked at Rohan.

'Sure thing! Goes without saying,' I said.

I had one more gift to give her, and this seemed like the perfect moment, but I also wanted to remain in the warmth of the hug, so I decided it could wait.

After some time, we started making plans about where we were going tonight. We left the choice to her, as she was the expert, and we were sure that she would be disappointed with our choices. While she was looking at places, Rohan texted Snehal about the plan and asked her to get ready and meet us at around six. Nikil had gone home the previous night, so it was just me, Alisha, Rohan, Prajwal and Snehal. Alisha finally settled on a place in Hinjawadi called FML (apparently, food music love).

Snehal called Rohan and asked him to pick her up from the hostel, so he left. As soon as Alisha stepped into the bathroom to freshen up, Prajwal and I went downstairs to get the things from the car, which we hid in the kitchen. I started writing below the photos – short descriptions like a cutie, the three musketeers, the first trip, the squad and so on. Since time was less, I wrote the first things that came to my mind. Meanwhile, Prajwal started to blow up the balloons. She came out of the bathroom and went to another room to change. We quickly kept the balloons and photos in the kitchen and locked it.

I kept the second gift at the door of the room she was in, along with a note and flowers. Meanwhile, Rohan and Snehal arrived. 'You guys didn't do all this on my birthday,' Snehal was mock-angry. 'Next year for sure,' Rohan promised. 'Keep your voice down or his surprise plans will fail.'

We went back to the room and waited for her to react.

The doorknob twisted. We stopped talking and leaned our ears in that direction. Suddenly, there was a shriek. 'Karna! Are you mad or what!'

We were all confused.

She came to the room wearing the jacket. 'You just gave me gifts in the morning, and now again! Why are you wasting all this money?'

I was confused and worried about what she would say about the photo frame and the photos themselves.

Suddenly, she hugged me. 'The jacket is nice. Thank you.' It was the same childish voice that drove me insane.

I smiled back. 'This is the last gift of the day.'

'I know,' she said, blushing. It felt like she knew about the other gifts, given that it was still some time before her birthday.

Prajwal and I needed an excuse to decorate the room, and it needed to be a strong one so that she wouldn't get a hint. He told her that one of his friends was going home, so we had to go say goodbye to him. 'You guys take a cab and go there. We will join you at FML. And we won't be late, promise.'

We left just before the cab arrival and parked Prajwal's car in a spot far away from our place. Then we waited for them to leave. To some extent, we were like cops waiting to catch the criminal in a thriller.

It took ten minutes. The moment their cab left and Rohan texted "All good to go", Prajwal and I ran like thieves do when the coast is clear.

I went to the kitchen and brought out all the balloons and the decorating items. Prajwal fixed the lights and clips alongside to stick the photos too. *Macha*', Prajwal said while clipping a photo, 'at least tell her today how you feel about her.'

'I plan to...but I don't want to spoil her birthday if this goes southwards.'

Hearing me, Prajwal held his head in his hand. 'You're never telling her, are you? All this decoration will be in vain.'

We had perfectly placed the 'Happy Birthday' letter balloons at the centre with tiny lights sparkling around in an arch and photos hanging from the wires. There were heart-shaped balloons on the floor and walls, giving the room a strawberry-red hue. Just as I was viewing our work, her call arrived.

'Where are you?' she yelled. 'If you don't come here in five minutes, don't come at all.' Saying that she hung up. We ran back to the car with a speed greater than that we had arrived in.

We reached FML at around 10:30. We were scared – well, technically, I was scared. But Prajwal was all chilled out. We went inside and saw her from afar. She was laughing about something and talking animatedly with Snehal and Rohan. We approached them, with a big smile on my face trying to figure out what excuse to offer this time.

'What were you guys doing?'

Before I could say anything, Prajwal said, 'Long story, will tell you later.' And before she could say anything, I said, 'Damn, beer is not at all chilled', and called the waiter, asking him to exchange those. She got up to answer a call from her mom and went outside to talk.

'*Waah*! You guys covered it up very well,' Snehal said. Prajwal beamed. 'That's what we brothers do.' He gave me a fist bump. Rohan called, '*Bhai*, I am also here, and held up both his fists, which Prajwal and I bumped with ours.

'Were you guys able to get everything ready?' Rohan asked.

'Yes! Everything is in place. Now it's just the wait for the clock to hit the twelve-hour mark.'

Alisha came back and we stopped talking about it. We proceeded to down a few drinks. There was no dance floor, which was a big relief for me; we just drank and talked. Rohan had asked the waiter to get the cake five minutes before 12. The waiter was on time. She blew on the candles and cut the cake while we sang happy birthday to her. We left the place at around 12:30, already excited for the next celebration.

C 102

On our way to C 102, we all acted normal, and she seemed to not even have a clue about anything. We let her open the door and turn the lights on. I started playing 'Waiting for Love' by Avicii, and we all shouted 'Surprise!' as her eyes eased to the lights.

She seemed elated, a wide smile spreading on her face. 'Thank you, guys.' And then her eyes widened with recognition. 'You were late because of this! It makes sense now...'

We had cake but had forgotten to get candles. Prajwal's lighter came to use. She blew on it and suddenly chirped, '*Aree gaov tho* (Start singing)!' We sang happy birthday again while clapping loudly.

Rohan brought the vodka shots. 'Oh yeah! Now the party starts, bitches!' she shouted. This was her line which was indicative of her mood to party like crazy. We gulped the vodka like water and lost count between dancing and drinking. In no time, everyone had gotten tired. We turned on the lights and played slower songs. Some of us sat on the floor, but Prajwal and Rohan were in no mood to stop since they were tripping on 'Apocalypse' by Cigarettes After Sex. Alisha and Snehal were enjoying their slow dance, mouthing the words of the music. This seemed like the perfect moment for me to give the final gift and stop them at their tracks – or dance.

I reached my cupboard, took it out, went back and handed the wrapped present to her. 'Karna, I knew you had one more gift to give me. How should I match all these on your birthday? It's only a week away!' she said.

'No need to match anything. Just wish me every birthday. That's all I ask.'

'You're so sweet!'

She started opening the gift. Once it was out, she was lost in it for a few seconds, but in those seconds, everything and everyone had silenced. Her eyes filled with tears. She turned around and grabbed anyone within her reach; I wasn't. She was crying now. 'Thank you guys...for everything. It wouldn't be the best college memories without you all.' She was embracing everyone in a group hug.

I took a cigarette and went to the balcony to smoke. Some unknown reason made me not want to be part of that hug. I kept thinking about how I was just a part of her best college memories, the same as others. I wanted her to not treat me as an element of her squad. What would have made my day was appreciation meant just for me. It would have meant more than any gift she could have given me on my birthday. Selfishly, I thought of how it was I who put in more effort in making her happy, but the credit always went to the group. Earlier I had been fine with it and hadn't taken it seriously. After all, we were a family of sorts. But now something else was going on in my mind. I had assumed that I was special to her. Maybe that had led me to expect things, which got me disappointed.

The curtain of the balcony was shoved aside. I was expecting one of the boys to join me for a smoke.

Hands grabbed my waist while her face reclined on my back. A cool breeze swept my hair as I almost melted in that hug, the best I had ever gotten.

'*Nayike*, you always make me cry doing such things, and then you suddenly vanish...'

Nayike was her way of showing love for me. It is Kannada for 'dog'. It was something endearing that she would say when she felt warm towards me. Only I used to get called by her like that, which was all I wanted in that moment...or perhaps I wanted more, but it was only a fleeting hope.

I tilted back with my left arm opened up. She moved around and was soon in my arms. It was all perfect. Out of the blue, I remembered that dinner date which had gotten cancelled; she had promised we would do that before leaving Pune.

'Alisha, what about that dinner plan?'

'I am sorry. So many things have happened this week. I so wanted to go out, but whenever I came around to this, something or the other popped up. I am sorry,' she pouted.

'Of course,' I replied sarcastically.

'What was that?'

'Nothing. It's just that I was very excited about it, and now I feel you didn't do enough from your end. You were never serious about it. It's making me sad right now.'

She stood silent for a while. Slowly, she said, 'Karna... I really did want to go to dinner with you. Don't say things like that!'

Her voice broke, and while her words flowed, so did her eyes. Seeing her like this made me feel terrible. I immediately became the person I was an hour ago. 'Sorry, I am an ass... I don't know where all that came from. Sorry, please don't cry.'

'Fucker, you treat me so special on every day and then you make me cry on my birthday. I hate you. I hate you so much.' She sobbed.

I took her in my arms and held her tight. 'I am really sorry...I really am. I said all of that aloud because my overthinking would have killed me otherwise. Now at least I have something to believe in. I am so sorry.' I kissed her on the forehead. 'Alisha, I promise I will never make you cry.'

She calmed down and looked up with her head bent back. Her lips were curved in a pout, and her hands were tightly wrapped around my back. I removed her hair from her eyes and tucked it behind her ear while my right hand was on her lower back. Our eyes were locked and lost in each other's words. My heart thudded so loudly that I was afraid she might hear it; it might have been a simpler way of telling her about my feelings.

but I held back and didn't say anything as I don't want to make it worse and didn't take a chance to make it better. later everyone came to the balcony and stood by the rail and enjoyed the cool wind and cherished the Pune life we had so far and it was last night for us together, bit an emotional scene but everything good or bad must always come to an end. so was our best memories of life together with the squad that had come to pull stop point. everyone talked about the best memories they had so far and after that, we had one final shot of vodka and called it a day.

CHAPTER IX

THE FINAL SURPRISE

The beginning of the end

An entire lifetime seemed to have passed in college. That life finally came to an end. I had three months after collage before stepping into the so-called money-making routine, in other words, the corporate job.

In that three- to four-month span, we met once a month. She got a job in Mumbai, and I went to Bangalore. There was not much scope for conversation between us after she joined the company and met new people while adjusting to a new city. Things kept her busy.

I hated my job, perhaps mostly because it was in Bangalore and not in Mumbai. Perhaps the job profile didn't suit me. Or perhaps these reasons were connected. Nevertheless, I quit after four months and started searching for a job in Mumbai. Overcoming my stupid luck, I was finally offered a position by a company and started the onboarding paperwork.

All I could think of was how to surprise her with the news. But my luck was having none of it. If I had declared it my worst enemy, luck had made me its favourite pawn.

They held my offer for a month. Then it was the same old 'Sorry, better luck next time.'

That made me sick. All my dreams about her, my job and my life, in general, seemed to lead to a one-way road with a block reading 'better luck next time.

March is her birthday month. We had made a pact that we would be there for her birthday every year no matter how busy we got in our lives.

I have two months before her birthday, two months left to get a job and surprise her, and along with that, to work on my book. Finally, for once, I will let her know how I feel about her and that she means the world to me. Here I am then, hoping for luck to be exhausted in its dirty game, to finally give in and say, 'Bro, I have played with you enough. Go live your life now as you planned.'

CHAPTER X

THE JUDGEMENT DAY

Rohan
<u>*The Judgement Day*</u>

After finishing my work, I was heading back to my room. As my Uber was waiting outside the office, I was in a bit of a hurry. I entered the lift when my phone started to ring. It was Karna. I didn't receive the call while I was in the lift, and it ended before I could come out. When I called him back, I met a busy tone. Once I got into the cab, he called again. 'Bhai, when are you coming to Mumbai? And what are we gifting her this time?'

'7th March, bro, early morning. About the gift...let's take her shopping there itself. It is the best we could do instead of surprising her with gifts. She may not like our choices also.'

'I was also thinking the same.'

'What about your book? Have you completed that book that you were planning to give to her on her birthday?'

'*Bhai*, almost done. It's just that before giving it to her, I am planning to give her a big surprise. Maybe she will like it, but I am sure she will get surprised.'

'She will surely not, bro. But tell me, what are you planning to surprise her with?'

'Remember, she used to tell us about her engineering friends? A group called 4A. Amar, Anirudh, Ayush and Alisha. She had once introduced Amar to me, and we met a couple of times. I have been in touch with him, so I told him I was planning that he, Anirudh, Ayush, and I would go and surprise her on her birthday. He thought it was a good idea and said he'd ask those two and let me know.

'Once they all agree, the plan would go like this. We will take a rental car from Hubli for two or three days. We will leave on the 7th night, and by the 8th morning, we will reach Lonavala. I will book a villa there. They will stay in Lonavala, and I will go to Mumbai and pick her up. Later we will leave Mumbai such that we reach Lonavala by late evening on the 8th. We will go to some restaurant. After spending some time, we will get her to the villa with her eyes blindfolded. The others will have decorated the hall by then and would be waiting for us with a cake. As soon as she takes off the blindfold and opens her eyes, we will shout "Surprise surprise!"

'So, what do you think? Will she get surprised?' Karna finally said.

'Bro, if I was a girl and her friend, I would've wished that she says no to you so I could have a chance with you,' I said jokingly.

'Rohan, please be serious. Tell me, will she like it or not?'

'She will get surprised for sure, like a hundred percent. But those friends...will they come and make it happen?'

'Amar is taking care of it. I am hoping they do.'

'Okay, let us assume everything goes as planned. What happens next?'

'After that, we will drink and have fun. The next day she has an office; her boss gave her only half a day's leave. She will go to the office in the afternoon and return in the evening. Till then we will wait for her in the apartment. Before that, I will give you my book with two letters written separately. You will give it to her after my departure and be with her till she finishes reading. You have to work from home till then. She will surely complete reading within three or four days. Give her the letters after she finishes the book.'

'Bro, this means I have to be there for more than a week. It's your birthday on the 16ᵗʰ, so that makes it ten days. My boss will kill me.'

'This is a matter of life, *bhai*. Manage things with your boss. You anyway have the WFH option.'

I was in a fix. It was pretty obvious that I was going to stay, but it was suddenly a ten-day plan. I thought for a while. Karna would do the same for me if I was in his position. I agreed. 'What next?'

'I will meet you guys after she returns from office. The three of us will go and have dinner. I will go to Lonavala after that and pick up her friends and come back to Hubli. We will come back on the day before my birthday. Till then I won't talk about anything with her. Only after that will we talk face to face. If she agrees, it will be the best gift anyone will have ever given me. If things don't work out this way, we will see...'

'I am not sure about what she will say, but I am sure that she feels the same way about you. She won't leave you after she finds out, I can give that to you in writing.'

'Hmmm... Let's hope for the best. We're meeting on the 6ᵗʰ of March then. Bye.'

I had reached my apartment. *How can a person be this positive for so long?* I wondered as I switched on the lights, and at some point, it gave me chills. *Let's just hope she is sensitive to his feelings.* I would be the happiest if things went as planned and I get to be part of such an amazing journey of love.

Touchwood.

On Her Birthday

Everything was going as planned. Karna managed to get Alisha's 4A group to come to Lonavala. She was more than surprised; although she had had some clues of her own, she hadn't even imagined or dreamt of this. She celebrated her birthday with them after eight years. She was shedding happy tears seeing them. I didn't know how he had managed to pull this off, but Karna being Karna set the bar high every time when it came to surprising her. Her tearful smile was his fuel, and he never missed an opportunity to please her.

Later, we took her back to Mumbai. She had to attend office. Although she was in no mood to go, her boss didn't give her a choice. She kept cursing her boss on the way back in the car. We reached her office directly. Karna had to go because he had to drop her friends back, and by the time she would come back from the office, he would be gone, so people were getting a bit emotional. Karna donned a smile on his face like always, but he was just one nudge away from crying. But as soon as he saw her watery eyes, his tough exterior gave way and he started crying like a child while hugging her. I had to be the adult and consoled them. She gave him a goodbye kiss on the cheek, saying, 'Come back soon.' 'I'm only one call away,' Karna said. She went to the office, and we went to her apartment to freshen up.

It was noontime. Karna was about to go back. He finally gave me his book, two copies, one for her and one for me. Along with that, he gave me two envelopes.

'After she finishes reading the book, give her the letter that has her name on it. Once she is done reading it, use your best judgment and see if she seems happy or sad. Only then give her the second envelope. If you think she is angry, it means I have hit the dead end. In that case, throw this letter away, and don't you even read it.'

'Bro, one second. How will I know how she feels? What if I misjudge her feelings?'

'You will get to know like always. You have always read her well, and I trust you to make the right decision. And now I need to go and pick her friends up who are waiting in Lonavala.' He sat in the car.

'Don't go yet,' I said. 'There's still some time. Let's go have lunch.' We went to Belapur and had lunch along with one pint of beer each. He was initially refused because of the drive, but I convinced him to try one pint at least.

When he was ready to drive, he seemed relieved and happy, like he had achieved something. Maybe he was thinking about future life if she should accept his proposal. I didn't say anything and let him revel in his thoughts. Again, I was amused with his positive thinking, so this is what I needed to comment upon.

'How do you manage to stay this positive even though there is a chance that it could go the other way? And what drives you to write a book, man? It's hard to push that determination continuously considering a 50–50 chance.'

'It's simple,' he said. 'You just have to close your eyes and imagine being with your loved one on a long drive, where she leans on your shoulder, and all of a sudden you feel that the road should be straight as long as possible because you don't want to disturb this posture by shifting gear or moving the steering wheel. It's this thought that keeps me up and running. Maybe it is called love, this ability to feel and see the positive things. Imagining a life where my person is with me every day gives me an immense amount of rush as if I could conquer the world. I guess it's all her...she is the key to everything for me.'

'Let's just hope everything goes right.' I had an important role here to play, so hoping for the best, I went back to her apartment and started thinking about when and how I should do what was expected of me.

As the time for her arrival was getting closer, I was getting nervous and almost dropped a text to Karna saying I couldn't do it. But somehow I managed not to do that, pacing up and down the room and constantly watching the wall clock. Suddenly, the bell rang. I immediately opened the door.

Seeing my face, she asked, 'What happened? You behave like you have seen a ghost.'

'Exactly,' I said to relieve my tension.

'*Harami*,' she said and gently patted me on the shoulder. The nervousness seemed to have disappeared for now. It felt like I had dodged the bullet there. She went to get freshened up.

'Shall we go out for a drink?' I asked.

'Like, now?'

'Yeah, I feel like drinking tonight.'

'Okay,' she shrugged. 'I will get ready then. Give me five.'

I had dressed up real quick and was sitting on the sofa with the book gift-wrapped and the letters in my pocket. It had been past five minutes and my pressure was building up.

'WHAT!!!' she screamed. I instantly rushed to the door. 'What happened, Alisha?'

There was no response. Suddenly, I could hear her crying. 'Open the door, please...' I pleaded. 'Tell me what's wrong.'

Slowly, she opened the door. Her eyes were red and swollen, her cheeks streaked with tears. She was trembling all over and yet surprisingly unmoving. I held her and shook her to elicit some reaction. Her face crumpled up and she started howling. All the worst possible scenarios were running in my mind as I kept asking her, 'Tell me! Tell me what happened for god's sake...'

'Karna...accident...'

She dropped to the floor with her head in her hands. Profound terror had overtaken me. I couldn't move at first. Somehow, I managed to run to the kitchen and bring her some water. I made her drink it, and then I took her phone and dialled the last number in the log. It was Amar. 'What happened?' I could barely ask as my voice shook. 'She is crying like anything here. What did you tell her?'

'Rohan...' he said in a very low tone. 'Karna got hit by a traveller while crossing the road. We were having tea on the other side. We are in the hospital now.'

Although my lips quivered trying to say something, my vocal cords had given up. I held her hand tightly and asked Amar to send us the hospital's location.

With that, I ended the call. I wanted to ask him how badly he had gotten hit and how serious the situation was, but I couldn't. All I could do was pray that it wasn't too bad.

Deep inside, both of us knew what the situation could be like. But we were hoping for fate to prove us wrong. 'It's a small accident, there's nothing to worry about. Now go wash your face.' I took her to the bathroom and splashed water on her face. Then I booked the cab and called Amar again. 'How serious was the accident?' After a pause, he said, 'Nothing serious. You guys just come here fast.'

'Bro, please tell me the truth. Alisha is not around. Tell me exactly how his condition is.'

'It was scary, the state in which we found him. He is doing poorly. Doctors aren't revealing much, but they are treating him in the ICU now. We are scared as hell, please come soon.'

Life had turned upside down. As I hung up, my legs fell short of strength, and I fell on the couch. Only a few moments ago I was sitting in the same place with a very different sort of nervousness. How drastically things change in minutes.

My hands touched against the gift-wrapped book. I closed my eyes. 'Karna, you can't do this to me, and like hell, you can do this to her,' I whispered. 'Don't you dare stop fighting. God, please give him strength.' I couldn't wait to take her to the hospital since I was sure she would be the ray of hope he needed to keep fighting.

We were in a cab and about to reach Lonavala. I saw his car parked at the side along with a traveller one. There were also a few cops, but I couldn't see clearly. The scene scared me as nothing had before. I saw her watching over the window, her tears pouring without break.

For some reason, I made a decision. I didn't know if it was right or wrong, only that I needed to do it. Immediately, I told her the reason that I wanted to go out and have a drink. 'Karna gave me this gift to give to you and two envelopes along with it, and I feel you should have it. He wanted you to read the book first and then the envelopes in order.'

She held the book and letters close to her heart. 'I knew he was writing about me, but I never thought he would complete it. But that fucker did. He always took care of me like a baby.' Her voice broke and she started sobbing again.

On reaching the hospital, we ran to the ICU hallway. Doctors were talking to her friends. The way their heads were bent only made my fear worsen.

'What did they say?' I asked them, panting loudly. Amar started crying. 'They say they have done everything possible, but he can't make it. He asked us to call his close ones.'

Alisha fainted, and her body fell limp against the wall. We sprinkled some water on her face and woke her up. By then, the doctors had shifted him to the normal ward. We could finally go see him. She was afraid, but I held her hand and took her in. He was in there with his head covered in a white bandage. One of his eyes was shut. With his other eye, he saw us and tilted his head. His lips moved, and he was smiling, a tear lingering on his cheek. By now, we were all sobbing loudly. Alisha walked towards him and held his hand.

Karna whispered something, so she moved closer to him to hear him better. We did too. '*Nayike*, why...crying? I...fine.'

She was horrified. Wiping her tears, she said, 'Why, Karna? You could have looked either way and crossed the road!'

Karna smiled again and nodded. Turning towards me, he said, 'Hero, what...up?' He saw the gift in my hand. 'Don't...give...' I saw how much effort it took him to speak. Every word came out between long breaths. It was as if someone had grabbed his words which he had to squeeze out.

Alisha came and snatched the book. She turned to look at Karna. 'I knew about the book, Karna, and now I am going to read it here itself.' She tore open the wrapper. The cover was her face, halfway in shadows, her pointed nose and sharp chin illuminated by the light. The title read ***Alisha, the Kohinoor in My Life.***

'Karna, I wanted to tell you that I think I am in lo—'

The machine beeped, hitting the flat line. 'Karna?' she cried out loud. 'No, no, no, no... Karna?! *Nayike*... I was saying something, wake up! Don't you dare leave me like this, you ass!'

She was thumping his chest with her fists. I grabbed her hands and tried to calm her down by patting her head. 'Wake him up!' she shouted. She was starting to faint again, so her friends gently carried her out.

I sat beside him. 'Bro,' I held his limp head. 'What should we do now? What friend do I have left now? Who will wake me at odd hours and cry about his crush? Who will share his feelings with me?' There was so much to be done. All I wanted was for life to go back to what it was in college. 'You left us midway, bro. I hate you. What about that two thousand that you owe me? You don't leave debts. Come back, bro...come back...'

After the Chaos

A week later, on March 16th, when the clock had just hit 12 midnight, Alisha, Snehal, Prajwal, Nikil and I, in her apartment, decided to celebrate Karna's birthday. He would have gone nuts if he was here seeing all of us turning up for his birthday. Perhaps a few of us would not have been here if he was with us; they would have wished him on a video call. As the saying goes, 'We don't value things until we have lost them.' We loved him; he was funny, caring, sensible...and whenever we imagine his face, it would always materialise with his constant smile. He was always smiling, our Karna. Only the close ones could tell what emotions lay behind that smile of his.

As we gathered around the cake and cut it, some of us were in tears while the rest were barely holding them back. We all had a glass of beer in our hands – his favourite, Ultra.

Prajwal stepped forward. 'I would like to say a few words about him.'

We remained silent and let him articulate what he wanted to say. 'When I first met him, he seemed silent and very shy. But as the days passed, I realised that he was an entirely different person. We became close in the second year; from friends, we became a family of sorts. He was the reason I met you all. Karna always cared about everyone, and I so wish God had taken care of him similarly. He went too soon. My brother, my friend. I will always feel his absence. Happy birthday, Karna.' He raised his beer in the air.

It was now Nikil's turn. 'One emotional fool, Karna. But he could adjust with anyone. We were both so different, and yet he became my best friend. Happy birthday, brother.' To lighten the mood, he added, 'By the way, it was I who made Ultra his favourite drink.'

We all smiled. Snehal walked in the centre. 'He was the most innocent person ever. It was so easy to be with him. That jolly face of his will be forever etched in my mind.'

'He will always be family to me,' I said. 'The brother I never had.'

Everyone had delivered their eulogies. We were now waiting for Alisha to say something and turned towards her. She remained silent. After a while, she said, 'Happy birthday, Karna.'

Later that day, everyone had returned to their respective places. Only Snehal, Alisha and I remained.

In the hospital, when she had fainted for the first time, I had kept the book and letters with me. Later, she only grabbed the book but forgot the letters.

As we sipped on our tea, a Snapchat notification arrived reminding us of Karna's birthday and asking us to send him a special emoji. Snehal and I acted like we hadn't seen it. When Alisha saw it, she closed her eyes and sighed. Then she turned towards me.

’Rohan, can you take me to Pune in the evening?‘

’Sure, but why?‘

’Snehal, come with me.‘

’Where would we be going?‘ Snehal asked.

’I will tell you on the way.‘

’Have you read the book that he gave you?‘ I asked.

She nodded. She had been calm throughout, and her reaction confused me. I had also read the book, and it had given me goosebumps. All that he had written about refreshed my memory. It reminded me of my first love back in my school days.

We sat there in silence.

’When we were in college, Karna wanted to have dinner with me. It never happened. And now there’s nothing that I regret more. On his birthday today, I want to make his wish come true. He had wanted us to have dinner at Marine Drive Restaurant in Pune.‘

’Yeah, I remember him telling me about it.‘

’You could have told me. Maybe things would have been different.‘

’Karna made me promise not to say anything. And he did ask you for it...twice, I guess. But you never went.‘

’I wanted to go with him, but in the end, things were moving so fast, with parties and then after-parties. He was part of it all. I had thought we could do it on the last day before leaving Pune, but some other things came up. I apologised for it.‘

’I know, but he was quite disappointed. Especially after the second time.‘

’Hmm... I feel so terrible. If I don’t do this today, I wouldn’t be able to live with myself.‘

’The cab is booked. It will be here by 4 in the evening.‘

We sat at two different tables. She sat alone while I and Snehal sat at a different table. She ordered two pints of beer and fries – Karna's favourite combo. I gave the envelopes to the server and asked them to give those to her.

She had kept one glass of beer on the other side of the table and the fries along with it. She clinked her glass to the one on the opposite side and started drinking. It was killing us to see her like this. Karna would have cried watching her gestures. But it had to be done,

so we didn't stop her.

As she was wiping her tears, the server handed her the letters. She looked at me, and I nodded, mouthing, 'Go ahead.'

Initially her head was rapidly moving from left to right, but then she slowed down, her eyes pausing at every word as if she didn't want the letter to end. When she finished, she signalled for us to join her. We took our seats beside the empty chair, where Karna would be sitting.

Alisha handed me the letter she had already read and was opening the second one. No sooner had she opened it than she broke down. 'Karna... he got the job in Mumbai...' Snehal held her head against her chest and then took her to the washroom. All I could feel was rage. If only he had been more careful. All that he had wished for was coming true.

I opened the letter.

The Proposal

Alisha,

Tum pehle itna khoobsurath thi ya

Waqt ne kiya koi haseen sitam!

'Isshhh kya filmy line maar rah hai!' You would be saying this. Ugh, forget I ever said it. It was just to break the ice.

It's difficult writing this down, as my palms are sweaty and I am shivering. But here goes...

You, Alisha, are a special person. Everyone says this to their loved one, but if they had met you and seen you from my eyes, and still thought others were special, they would be lying for sure. The way you smile, talk and dance can make anyone lose their mind. But what I have fallen for, apart from those talents of yours, is the way you care about people close to you. Despite being busy, you make sure to always make everyone in the room happy so that they don't get FOMO. That right there is what you're top-notch at. And for a fact, I know you know I know that it is what you love doing (see, you're making me drop FRIENDS references).

Before you happened in my life, it was bland and monotonous; think of Ranbir Kapoor going to office in Tamasha. Wake up, go to college, come back, watch a show, eat, repeat. But after you came and allowed me to be your friend, I felt that there is more to life than my boring routine. Since then, good things just got better and bad things didn't seem so awful, I have aspired to spend all my time with you. I was so happy that my life span might have gotten increased by a few years. If we both start living together, I might even attain immortality!

They say opposite forces attract. It is the law of nature, and you, Alisha, are that force in my life.

You talk like there's no tomorrow and I am happy to listen to you all my life.

You love to dance, and I love to watch you dance.

Your quick temper and my monk-level patience make us a perfect pair.

I guess what I am trying to say is...

Dear Alisha,

I will be Chandler if you be my Monica

I will be Leonard if you be my Penny

I will be Jake if you be my Amy...

Answer me, so that someday who knows people might say:
I will be Karna if you be my Alisha.

I was still thinking about the letter when Alisha and Snehal returned from the washroom and i was thinking about weather to give the second letter or not but by seeing her condition i though its best if she didnot read it and decide to keep it to myself. she came and sat on karns place and started drinking his beer, almost tearing up again.

Did she have feelings for Karna? I wondered. Regardless, it was too late.

If you are reading this, remember that life's too short to wait for the perfect moment or create a perfect scenario to do what you have to do.

Keep it simple. If there's someone you secretly like, tell them. You never know, maybe they feel the same about you. But always bear in mind to be sincere and give them space. Let them make their decision at their pace because we can't force them to love us back. But what we can do is focus on our behaviour. So we must stay positive.

Alisha stopped crying, and Snehal accompanied her out of the restaurant. I told them I would join them in a minute. After they left, I took the chair beside the one he was supposed to be in.

'Bhai, Alisha nae tho tera ek wish pura karliya and mera kya bhai, I failed to fulfil mine, which is setting you up with her. I was so close, man. And I truly believed it would have happened. But fate interfered and your story just turned out like the Kohinoor Diamond, that it does not stay where it should have been.

'But I promise I will make your dream to be a writer come true. This book will reach thousands of people and make them believe in love again.'

I looked up at the sky. 'Happy birthday, Karna.' I took a sip of his beer. 'We will be here for you, every year, all of us. We miss you, bro, and you'll always be among us.'

THE END